DESIRE ME ALWAYS

By Tiffany Clare

Desire Me Now
Desire Me More
Desire Me Always

DESIRE ME ALWAYS

TIFFANY CLARE

AVONIMPULSE
An Imprint of HarperCollinsPublishers

DESIRE ME ALWAYS. Copyright © 2015 by Tiffany Clare. All rights reserved under International and Pan-American Copyright Conventions. By payment of the required fees, you have been granted the nonexclusive, nontransferable right to access and read the text of this e-book on screen. No part of this text may be reproduced, transmitted, downloaded, decompiled, reverse-engineered, or stored in or introduced into any information storage and retrieval system, in any form or by any means, whether electronic or mechanical, now known or hereafter invented, without the express written permission of HarperCollins e-books.

EPub Edition NOVEMBER 2015 ISBN: 9780062380487

Print Edition ISBN: 9780062380470

AM 10 9 8 7 6 5 4 3 2 1

For Scott

CHAPTER ONE

Highgate, London, 1881

This wedding was happening today.

The wedding of all weddings, even if it was planned in haste, Amelia Grant had managed to snag one of London's most sought-after bachelors.

Amelia screwed up her nose as she stared at the sad sight of her reflection in the dressing table mirror. It was a shame she looked the way she did, because it quelled some of her confidence on a day that was supposed to be special.

An abrasion—still raw and tender—ran three inches along her hairline and across her temple. There was a jagged, slightly swollen cut at the side of her mouth that hurt if she smiled too brightly. But her face was far from the only part of her body to have sustained injury.

The rope burns that wrapped around her wrists were a constant reminder of just how helpless she'd been at the hands of two madmen. Where her collarbone was bared above her chemise, deep purple bruises marred her pale skin.

Frustrated by the dreadful vision she made, Amelia looked down at the array of cosmetics Lady Burley had obtained for her, the sole woman to see the horrors of Amelia's physical appearance. Lord and Lady Burley had traveled to Highgate to negotiate the purchase of some of the properties Nick had taken over with the Caldon Manor acquisition. Amelia truly appreciated Lady Burley's kindness since the *incident*.

Amelia opened up jars of cream and powder; she wasn't sure where to begin, as she'd never worn cosmetics—that simply was not something a lady should wear.

Carefully—and a little skeptically—she dabbed some of the creamy concoction on her bruised cheek with the tip of her finger; she was surprised by how well it covered the unsightly mark. Having her injuries made invisible—or near to—had her lip curling up in a smile.

The day was already looking brighter, and for the first time this morning, fluttering of nervousness and excitement snaked through her body.

With her face looking somewhat normal, Amelia loosened her plaited hair and let it fall in dark waves around her face and shoulders. She was unsure how she should arrange it as her hands tired quickly—a result of being trussed up like a Christmas goose during her capture. Twirling the strands about her hand, she twisted it low at her nape.

A light tap sounded on Amelia's chamber door, startling her enough that she dropped her hair.

"It's Lady Burley."

"Please come in," Amelia called back.

Lady Burley walked into Amelia's room. The woman was beautiful and regal as ever.

"I came to see what assistance I might provide," Lady Burley announced. "I even brought maids with me."

It was a kind gesture that lifted Amelia's spirits greatly.

"How wonderful," she said.

Lady Burley wore a genuine smile that was hard not to reciprocate as Amelia looked at her in the glass above her dressing table. With her dark hair and freckled complexion, Lady Burley looked more like a country girl who spent her days outdoors than the countess of a prominent—and very business-savvy—earl. Regardless, there was an air of elegance that swathed the woman and made Amelia slightly envious that she did not have the same refinement. Even though Amelia was the daughter of an impoverished earl and had a lady's upbringing, she had never had an opportunity to practice and perfect the social graces she'd learned as a child.

"Your kindness means a great deal to me, Lady Burley."

"You are marrying my husband's dearest friend," Lady Burley said. "It is only natural for friendship to blossom between us. And it's hard to resist some early celebration for the day."

"And were I not marrying Nick?" Amelia didn't intend to sound quite so cynical, but she'd had few people she could rely on growing up and not one steady friend in the whole of her life.

"Impossible. It was only a matter of time before Nick walked you down the aisle. He's been besotted since he first introduced you at the Langtry dinner."

The Langtry was London's finest hotel and owned by Hart, another of Nick's friends. Dining there had been the first social function she'd attended with Nick, and it had been a night never to forget.

It had been a night of firsts.

A jolt of shame and embarrassment flushed through Amelia for her indiscretions. "I hadn't realized we were so…obvious."

"I doubt everyone present was as observant," Lady Burley assured her. "You shouldn't let it worry you. You will be married by day's end."

Still, she didn't want assumptions about their hasty marriage. Nick had obtained special permission and a permit to marry without the proper banns being read. Yet such a precipitous move would have members of society wondering whether or not she was with child, which she was not; Nick had a special tea made for her daily to ensure it. All assumptions aside, she hoped everyone saw how much she loved Nick and how much he loved her. She hated to be judged harshly.

Lady Burley reached for Amelia's brush and separated her hair in four parts before raking the bristles through it. "I meant what I said; you shouldn't worry what others believe. Who are they to judge Mrs. Riley? You'll be richer than most lords and ladies—they do despise when those they deem beneath them are more successful—and you are far kinder than the majority of them." Lady Burley clucked her tongue as she ran her fingers through Amelia's hair, pulling out any knots that remained. "You know…this is the last thing you should be thinking about when today is meant for celebration."

A maid entered carrying a silver tray with two glasses of champagne in perfect timing of Lady Burley's words. Lady Burley picked up both of the bubbling glasses, handing one to Amelia. They clinked their glasses together. Amelia set her glass down after the first sip. If she drank the whole glass, she doubted she'd be able to walk down the aisle straight.

"I never imagined I would marry for necessity," Amelia admitted.

The necessity being that they were known to have shared a bed the night of her kidnapping.

"Or in haste." Amelia didn't think that it would matter whether they waited a week or a month, as long as they married. Apparently to Nick, it did matter. Not that she was complaining.

She wanted Nick to be her husband. Wanted to be addressed as Mrs. Riley. She wanted the world to know how much she loved him.

"Nick is a determined man once his mind is made up," Lady Burley said.

Which was true.

Amelia's lips tilted up in a careful smile. Nick would not take no for an answer once he'd asked for her hand in marriage. That determination was part of what she loved so much about him. But was that enough to bind them together for the rest of their lives? They had known each other for only a short time.

Surely all brides had these worries before making that final leap toward marriage.

Amelia held out some hairpins for Lady Burley. "I cannot express how grateful I am for all the help you have given me, but I can arrange my own hair," Amelia said.

"Not on your own wedding day. Besides, I am only starting your hair." Lady Burley plucked the pins from Amelia's hand. "Getting the front just perfect. One of the maids has gone in search of a few hairpieces to hold the veil in place."

"There's a veil?"

This was…unexpected. Amelia eyed her blush-pink day dress spread out over her bed. A veil would not suit the sunny color she'd chosen for today.

"How can a wedding be complete without a veil? Nick commissioned the local milliner to make it. She said your husband was in luck that she had lace on hand. Victoria would have made it, had she had more time, but she did ensure your dress arrived this morning and in time for the big day."

And there was a dress?

Amelia's eyes filled with tears. All these people had come together to make this day perfect. They must love Nick a great deal. It was no surprise to her when his great accomplishments and successes were from lifting up people in dire circumstances and giving them a chance to prove their worth and ability—her included among those ranks.

Then it dawned on her who had made the dress, and her expression changed to one of suspicion.

"You said Victoria made the dress?"

Surely Lady Burley was mistaken about Nick's ex-lover wanting to help out in any way.

"She did. It was fortunate that she had your measurements on hand."

This news stunned Amelia. While the woman had reluctantly made her dresses more suiting to her role as Nick's secretary and companion at dinner parties, it was with great *reluctance* and, Amelia was sure, Nick's insistence. While there was no love lost between her and Victoria, she couldn't refuse the gift. Not when she suspected that Nick pulled strings to make their wedding day special.

"And here I thought I would wear my best day dress for the occasion," Amelia said. "What does it look like?"

"I know you will be pleased." Lady Burley stuck another pin in Amelia's hair. "Victoria's done a wonderful job in such a short time."

"Is she here?" The venom that filled Amelia's voice was undeniable. Lady Burley was either clueless to Amelia's feelings, or she gracefully chose to ignore the undertone of dislike Amelia had difficulty hiding.

"She couldn't leave the store today, and I guarantee you that she had no desire to see Nick married to another."

A horrible thought struck Amelia.

"Does she still love him?" Amelia slapped her hand over her mouth. She couldn't believe she'd spoken without thought of what she was asking. One didn't fall easily out of love, so likely, Victoria loved and wanted Nick to herself.

"I forget how little experience you have with London's social politics. There is no doubt in my mind that there is love in the form of friendship between them, but Victoria…" Lady Burley tapped her lips in thought. "How does one delicately say it?"

Amelia stared back at Lady Burley's reflection in the mirror, unsure of to what she was alluding.

"Victoria's one and only true love is power. She has to be in complete control in every situation. Actually, you could equate her to the feminine version of Nick. And we women well know that what is highly regarded in men going on about their business is not looked upon brightly when women take on those same characteristics, especially in the union of marriage."

Amelia had to bite her tongue. Her main dislike for Victoria was rooted in jealousy, as Victoria had been Nick's lover at one time. But they had broken off before Amelia had ever met Nick. Being so different, as compared to Victoria, made her feel somewhat inferior. Hearing Lady Burley say Victoria was an equal to Nick made her cross. Amelia was an equal to Nick, and she would have it no other way.

Amelia's emotions got the better of her, and her eyes filled with tears. Those tears weren't for Victoria but for the fears that had been building up these past few days. A fear that the wedding was all a dream, that Nick was only an imagination, considering how fast everything had happened between them. And the biggest of the fears was that she'd wake up any moment and be back at home in Berwick with her brother lording over her, filling her life with the misery she'd grown used to while living under his heavy hand.

The brush stilled as Lady Burley met Amelia's gaze in the mirror. "Oh, Nick didn't tell you any of this. Forgive me for my forwardness."

How Amelia kept her tears from falling was nothing short of a miracle. "It's not that. I truly appreciate your honesty. It's just that I have been the proverbial watering pot since…"

She didn't want to discuss her kidnapping. Not now, not today. Maybe not ever.

"I'm not sure why Nick wants to marry me when it seems that bad luck has followed me from the onset of our first meeting."

"The heart knows what it wants."

"Does it?"

"You have been through more than most people could handle. Do not believe for one moment that you have to explain yourself to anyone. Nick wouldn't have offered marriage if he wasn't willing to make the commitment required for such a momentous promise. Now, let's focus on the day ahead and not the past that led you here." Lady Burley pulled something from her pocket and revealed the prettiest hair combs Amelia had ever laid eyes upon. "Would you prefer the pearls for your hair or the gold studs?"

Lady Burley's lightened the mood with her good humor.

It wasn't that Amelia was having second thoughts of marrying Nick; far from it. She just hated the fact that his hand was forced and that he was marrying her out of necessity. Perhaps it was natural for doubts to linger after a life-changing event. Perhaps this was all part of marriage.

The only thing that should be occupying her thoughts was happiness. After today she would be Mrs. Nicholas Riley. She had wanted this from the beginning. Nick had been forthcoming in his desire to keep her as his own, and she was making the irrevocable step in making that happen. Who was she to refute his claim over her when his determination to possess her sent a thrill of giddiness through her?

Amelia picked up her champagne glass and took another sip, a smile lighting up her whole face. Mrs. Nicholas Riley indeed.

Today was the day.

The day Nick Riley would lay claim to his bride in front of his friends, in front of a God he had trouble believing in, considering the life he came from, and in front of all the eyes in the church that glanced at him with a gamut of emotions—from envy to fear...and respect.

Over the past few days, he'd heard the townsfolk's gossip. The talk had been all about Amelia's kidnapping, her injuries, and his inability to save her before she'd been harmed.

That failure was his alone.

One for which he would atone for the rest of his life. It was his fault he'd brought her to this godforsaken village, insisted on her attendance, insisted she sleep next to him in his bed. He'd sullied her reputation with his greed to have her at his side and his need to possess her.

But today...

Today would make it right.

Their union would silence all the wagging tongues. Let them move on to someone else. Amelia hated it, and he hated that he'd been the cause of it.

Nick never imagined himself married. Whether or not this public ceremony was necessary, Nick had always been a private person. Putting on this display eviscerated him on some level. Even his friend Landon, the Earl of Burley, had advised him to take this step.

One of the clergymen said something, but Nick had been too focused on his thoughts to catch his words. "My apologies; my mind is elsewhere. What was it you said?"

"I said the townsfolk are looking forward to your influence in the area."

Of course they were, though Nick didn't say this to the clergyman. He had every intention, with his friend Landon, to make the Highgate area thrive as it never had before, since he was no stranger at making something out of nothing. In addition to that, changing this village for the better was not something at which Nick would fail, as the people here had proved worthy of all the help they could get after their assistance with rescuing Amelia. He was indebted to them all.

"I have a great many plans for this place." Nick hadn't discussed building the school with anyone outside his friends and sister. And it was none of their damned business until it became critical to hire on help to rebuild the old manor house he had bought for that very purpose.

First, Nick had to deal with Shauley, the man directly involved in kidnapping Amelia. Shauley had been the bloody mastermind behind it all, striking indirectly at Nick but knowing how to cripple him most effectively. Nick's and Shauley's paths hadn't crossed since they were youths, since their loss of innocence. Just recently, Shauley seemed to have some vendetta against Nick and his purpose for buying the Caldon Manor.

After today, Amelia would have the protection of the name on which Nick had built his reputation and empire. No one would have cause to harm her again.

Except Shauley.

Shauley would still see his wife as a target, as a challenge to be conquered, and all in the name of getting back at Nick for an old feud. Nick had every intention of finding the oily bastard, and he didn't care if he had the full letter of the law behind him in seeking that justice.

No one touched what belonged to him. It was as simple as that.

If Shauley showed his face again, Nick's old foe would not live to tell about it.

Hart elbowed Nick in the side, drawing his attention away from his troubled mind.

"You look tense. What has your thoughts?" Hart asked.

Hart had an uncanny skill at reading people. Nick disliked it when his friend used that skill on him. Not that he would explain what he was thinking.

"It's been an eventful week."

"Don't tell me you're getting cold feet for your lovely bride? I'll be happy to step in if you are."

Nick gave his friend a sidelong look, full of annoyance. "If you offer to step in my shoes again, I'll personally throw you out of this church."

His friend merely smiled at the threat, as if it were a dare. "Now you're back to your old glowering self."

Nick didn't think so.

Today was nothing more than a formality. He knew that this was something Amelia wanted and needed to save the last shreds of her reputation. But he already considered them irrevocably bound.

He checked his fob watch again. What was taking his bride so long this morning? Perhaps she had the jittery feet? It was up to Landon to get her here, as he'd volunteered to give her away. And who was Nick to refuse after all the earl had done for them? Landon had been the first to offer his assistance when Amelia was kidnapped, and he saw what that bastard Shauley had done to Amelia.

And through the whole ordeal, not once did Landon judge Nick's actions. Or comment on the indiscretions Nick had committed with Amelia. Nor was there disapproval from Landon's wife, Meredith, who had spent the morning assisting his bride in getting ready. He tucked his watch back into his waistcoat, determined to show the world that he was not worried Amelia might change her mind and leave him standing at the altar.

That wasn't something she would do.

She was steadfast, loving. Far more than Nick deserved.

A strange emotion filled Nick's chest, something sentimental—and not something familiar to him. Everything was different with Amelia. She made him a different person, a better man. Not having her in his life was something he simply couldn't contemplate.

All he knew was that without her...he was nothing.

The door at the front of the church opened, allowing the morning sun to light the path his bride would take. Hart put his arm around Nick's shoulders and physically turned him toward the minister at the front. Nick nearly glared at his friend, but he recalled some superstition that said it was bad luck for the future husband to watch his bride walking toward him. So he inhaled deeply and waited.

This was finally it...

A new beginning for them both.

Chapter Two

Even after the early morning hours spent in Lady Burley's company, Amelia still had trouble swallowing the fact that today was the day she would become Mrs. Riley.

Married! *Her!* It was definitely not something she had ever expected when she'd run away from home and come to London. The thought hadn't even crossed her mind.

That wasn't to say that when she was a little girl she hadn't dreamed of *her* perfect wedding. She recalled with fondness walking down an imaginary aisle, using rows of wildflowers that grew in the countryside as her path. Wreaths of flowers crowned her head and wrapped around her waist like a medieval princess as she stepped toward her very own imaginary knight in shining armor.

It amazed her every day that she'd found that knight in Nick, as he was forever rescuing her.

Her stomach turned over, uneasy and nervous, excited and so ecstatic she thought she might burst with the happiness that infused her. Permanent goose bumps marched the length of her arms, and her heart intermittently raced between every breath she took.

The fact that she was walking down the aisle toward Nick did nothing to settle the anxiety that strummed through her the moment the church doors opened.

At least thirty sets of eyes were focused on her, all present to witness her and Nick's marriage. How Nick managed to invite so many of the townsfolk in the five days it had taken to prepare for the occasion was nothing short of a miracle. And having so many people here made her feel immense guilt at having avoided them prior to the wedding.

The whole situation seemed unreal, and she wanted to pinch herself just to be sure today was real, that it truly was happening. As she and Nick grew closer, this was exactly what she wanted. Marriage to a man she loved. The only man with whom she had ever fallen in love, which wasn't to say that she was long in the tooth, just…inexperienced. There had been very few good examples of kind and caring men where she'd grown up.

Amelia tightened her grip on the Earl of Burley's arm. From the moment he learned of her and Nick's engagement, he had insisted on walking her down the aisle. It was a kind gesture, as her father was dead and couldn't give her away to the man she loved. Amelia had been grateful for Lord Burley's offer and delighted that he wasn't the only person to offer. Nick's other friend, Hart, had requested to fill the role. She'd met Hart on only a few occasions, but he was always kind to her.

As they headed toward the front of the church, Nick already faced the minister who would marry them. Amelia couldn't help but wonder if the minister's willingness to assist in their special marriage license stemmed from pity, but she banished the thought before it took root and led her down another path of doubt. Lady Burley was right. Today was a special day—one for celebration and not a time to focus on bad memories.

Amelia focused on the minister, who had a ring of gray hair around his head that made him look like a friar of long-past years. His eyes were blue and twinkling in welcome. His smile was gentle and beckoned her closer.

Her stomach was a jumble of butterflies.

Sensing her unease, Lord Burley patted her arm reassuringly. She wished that was all the comfort she needed and forced herself to take long, steady breaths to keep from fainting.

It would be the height of embarrassment to have to use smelling salts to revive the bride. That thought made her chuckle and helped to keep her mind fixed on the finish line.

Nick turned to look at her, and the breath stilled in her lungs. His gray gaze reassured her and chased away the last of her qualms.

He didn't take his eyes off her. There were so many emotions swirling between them that she was sure everyone in the church *felt* the love radiating outward. Another of her breaths hitched, and Nick gave her a wicked smile before he faced the minister again.

Nick Riley would be her husband.

Husband!

As they neared the front of the large church, so grand for such a small affair, she turned to face Lord Burley, tears of happiness in her eyes. Lord Burley left her veil in place and gave her arms a gentle squeeze, the faint outline of a smile tugging at his lips.

"I hope you find the same happiness I have found in marriage," he said, his voice quiet, the words meant for her alone. Then, a little louder, he said, "If Nick gives you any difficulties, I'll be sure to straighten him out."

Amelia ducked her head, embarrassed, and hoped only a few people heard Lord Burley's comment. She would work out her own problems and insecurities with Nick directly. What they shared was private and for them only.

"Thank you for your generosity," she said faintly.

He leaned in close enough to whisper in her ear. "It is my pleasure. And you make a lovely bride."

Without further ado, Lord Burley turned her toward the front so the ceremony could begin and remained close to her left side, to bear witness to her and Nick's union.

So many thoughts went through her mind that she didn't so much as hear a word the minister uttered, only watched his lips move.

When Nick said "I will," she forced herself to focus. To listen to the words that would bind them for eternity.

All she could hear was an incessant buzzing in her ears, not absorbing any of the words the minister said, and then Nick was turning her toward him, his warm hand infusing her chilled one, not that he could tell, since she was wearing gloves, but his body heat wrapped around her like a blanket on a cold night.

In that moment where he held her hand tenderly, everything grounded in reality.

Everything was *right*.

"Wilt thou serve him, love, honor, and keep him in sickness and in health; and, forsaking all others, keep thee only unto him, so long as ye both shall live?" the minister asked of her.

She did not hesitate. "I will."

This man standing before her held her whole heart in his hands. That was how much she loved him—and she trusted him to keep her heart safe. She only had eyes for Nick at that point. It was as though only the two of them existed in the church.

Nick took her arm as the church clerk led them over to the signing table. Amelia picked up the pen and wrote her true name for the last time.

Amelia Celina Montgomery Somerset. The Somerset name was dead after this. In twenty-five years, that name had brought her more misery than joy. She could move on and forget all the ugliness of her past. And more than anything, she was glad to say good-bye to her position as the daughter of an earl and the obligation she felt holding that title.

She was free. Free from the duties of her old life. Free from the life that had been her prison for far too long.

She was now Mrs. Nicholas Riley. And nothing gave her greater joy than repeating her new name to herself.

Nick took the pen from her hand and repeated the process. When he turned to her, his hand tenderly cupped the side of her face over the veil. She wanted to kiss him and claim him in front of everyone present, but she could not be so bold in a house of God. Nor did she wish to reveal the damage of her brief imprisonment, still visible on her face—the cosmetics only dulled them to the eye—but safely hidden by her veil.

"You are the most beautiful bride I've ever laid eyes upon," Nick said, and it melted her heart to hear those words.

Nick's hand slid away from her face to grasp her hand. He led her out of the church. His focus was solely on her, as though she were the only person to look at—as though it was only the two of them here witnessing this great event.

A carriage waited just outside, ready to take them back to the inn. As they made their way to the open barouche, guests threw seeds and nuts over their heads that rained upon them in a rite of fertility. It shouldn't surprise her that everything down to the finest detail had been planned for them while she hid in her room, ashamed that she had once again been the victim of another's hatred.

This one moment of normalcy brought more tears to her eyes.

Her wedding day proved to be the most perfect day in her life.

Before she knew it, Nick was handing her up into the carriage, pulled by two white geldings, champing at their bits to be given free rein.

"How ever did you procure them?" She leaned forward, wishing for a better look at the beautiful animals, wishing she could touch them in all their majesty.

Nick hauled her down next to him on the soft velvet seat and pressed his fingers to her veil-covered lips. "We didn't have time to plan a wedding more deserving—"

"Nick…"

"It's a gift. One of many I intend to shower you with."

Amelia lowered her gaze, but she couldn't hide from Nick for long; his fingers were beneath her chin, lifting her face, forcing her to look at him and see the truth in his eyes.

"Don't shy away from me, Amelia."

"Today has been everything I ever wished for—and everything I never imagined possible. I'm overwhelmed by the emotions flooding me. By the love I feel for you...by everything. Oh, Nick, today has been so perfect I can't find the right words of gratitude."

"Words aren't needed."

Nick's hands gathered up the lace of her veil. Amelia grasped his wrist before he could reveal her face. The carriage hadn't yet moved, and she wasn't ready to share her wounds with the world, even though it was only a matter of time before she would have to face all the kind people who had attended their wedding.

"I will kiss my bride and claim you in front of our friends and guests."

Amelia gave a sidelong glance toward their audience, waving good-bye and cheering for them. What did she have to lose in ceding to Nick's one wish?

"Trust me," he said.

Nick's hands engulfed hers, and he lowered them to her lap, quashing her efforts to try to pull the veil back in place. He used his free hand to gather up the delicate gauze. As the last bit of Chantilly lace cleared her mouth, Nick laid his lips upon hers.

There was latent promise in the fold of his mouth over hers. It was like he was daring her, pushing her boundaries to see just how far she'd go. Would she deny herself something she wanted as much as he did? If she were a braver person, she would have lifted her veil in front of the guests, but she still wasn't ready to take that step. Instead, she pulled away, thankful the veil hid her furious blush from everyone who cheered them on.

"Wave good-bye to our guests, Amelia. I'm about to steal you away for what remains of the week."

"The week?" Panic set in.

"You're my wife." Nick turned his steady gaze on her, looking at her like he wanted to eat her up. "No one will judge us for not coming out of our room for the foreseeable near future."

Amelia laughed, though nerves might have caused her reaction more than mirth of the situation. "You have a wicked sense of humor and a devil of a tongue to tease me so. In case you have forgotten, our wedding dinner is planned for this evening," she reminded him.

"I don't tease. I promise. Dinner is something we can worry about much later." Nick leaned in and kissed her again.

As the horses pulled the barouche forward, Nick sat down beside her and hauled her onto his lap. She went with a squeal of delight. And they both waved to the guests that still stood outside the church.

Nick took one of her hands and pulled off her glove. He kissed the inside of her wrist, eliciting from her a sound crossed between surprise and desire.

"I want to take you here and now," he said. "I would if we didn't have so many witnesses."

His directness sometimes had a way of throwing her off balance, and it took a bit to mumble a response. "You say such bold and wicked things, husband."

"There's not a person in this world that I care for as I do you. And now, you are *officially* mine." His hand shamelessly curled around her ribs, his thumb brushing the underside of her breast as he held her close.

Amelia curled one arm around his shoulder. "And I adore you above all. I would not have married you otherwise."

Nick pressed her back against the bench, holding himself above her with a look in his eyes that almost dared her to stop him. "Do you honestly believe you had a choice in the matter?"

It was not a question. He was making a statement.

She shook her head. Marrying him had been the one thing she wanted from him as much as she wanted his commitment and love. When she thought about the past few weeks, she couldn't believe her luck in finding a man she adored and loved so much.

"Anyone can see what we are doing." Including the driver, though that didn't need to be said aloud, for he was thankfully facing the open road and seemed to be ignoring them.

"Let them all know I'm enamoured of my new wife. That I can't keep my eyes off you, let alone my hands." He lowered his face, his lips hovering above hers. "Or my mouth. I want to kiss every blushing part of your body and drag my tongue around every curve of skin and taste the pleasure you feel."

Hearing those daring words tumble so easily from his lips should have her pushing him away, but she liked his strength and virility so strong above her. Nick wasn't the kind of man to lie, and it wasn't above him to take whatever he wanted when he wanted it.

She nudged his arm. "You are a beast."

"I like the ring of that," he said with a growl.

"You will have to prove that point when we are ensconced in our bedroom," she teased. The simmering look in his eyes told her he would show her what he'd said and so much more.

Nick sat on the bench beside her, their thighs brushing. He looked like a man deprived of the one thing he wanted. She was glad that was her.

They remained in companionable silence the rest of the short ride back to their lodgings. Nick's hands rubbed small circles at the base of Amelia's back. His intent to claim her lips—and her body—was clear in his gaze. He only broke eye contact with her when the carriage stopped outside the inn.

Amelia took his hand on her descent. Her feet didn't have time to touch the ground before Nick swooped her up into his arms.

"Put me down." She was laughing as she made her request. "I feel absolutely ridiculous."

"I plan to carry you over every threshold in this house and do not plan on setting you down until you are in my bed."

She grinned. "You mean *our* bed."

"Yes, *our* bed. No walls will ever set us apart again."

Nick practically ran into the inn, but just before they hit the stairs that led up to their room, Amelia placed one hand over the side of his face. She turned him enough that she could kiss him full on the mouth now that they were in the relative privacy. Though their kiss was chaste, it stirred desire deep in her belly.

When their lips parted, Nick took the stairs two at a time to their room, easily opening the door and then kicking it shut behind them. She was holding on for dear life by the time they entered their bedchambers. She was laughing so hard that her ribs ached in her tightly laced corset. But that laughter died in her lungs when he set her down on the bed.

Nerves assailed her every sense. Her reaction seemed ridiculous considering everything they'd already done. But *this* was their wedding night. She didn't need to be a virgin to be anxious about what the night would bring.

"Do you suppose they will know what we are doing?" she asked shyly.

"I should hope so." Nick grinned wickedly as he leaned over her.

His lips were a warm, teasing breath away. Now she could do what she'd been dying to do since she'd seen him standing in the church this morning. She brushed her lace-covered lips over his and pulled away. It was a teasing touch.

"You shouldn't say such things." Secretly, she hoped he'd say the wickedest of things for the rest of their days.

"It's our wedding night. It would be odd if we spent the rest of our afternoon in the company of our guests when I can think of many better ways to utilize our time."

"But your friends are here to spend the evening in celebration with us. It makes me feel as if we are doing something wrong."

Nick gathered up the delicate material of the veil, finally revealing her face; though he was well aware of the wounds she carried from *that* night.

His thumb traced the faint bruise near her lip and then the jagged half-healed cut along her hairline. "You have nothing to feel guilty about. The night is ours, and everyone knows that."

"And neither do you." They both knew she was referring to the abuse she had suffered. It was no more her fault than his and that he felt the slightest bit of guilt bothered her so viscerally it made her heart ache for him.

Amelia clasped her hands around his, bringing his knuckles to her mouth to press her lips against them tenderly. It was in moments like this when she could pretend there were no secrets between them.

Nick's hand slid over her face and held onto the back of her head as he angled her face enough that he could devour her mouth with his—though he was careful with her damaged lip. Curling his other arm around her waist, he pulled her along the length of his hard body, crushing them together. The air whooshed from her lungs, and she hadn't realized just how desperate she was to be so close to him until this moment.

Nick lifted the wreath of orange flowers holding the veil down while she used her free hand to pluck the pins from the edge of the delicate material. The little pieces of metal clinked against the hardwood floor one at a time.

When the band atop her head came loose, she tried to pull it away, but it got caught in the intricate weaves that curled her hair into place.

She laughed at the absurdity of the situation, and Nick's mouth was suddenly absent as he spun her around, placing her back against his chest so he could carefully work the veil free from her hair.

"Not one hair on this beautiful head will be hurt. I'm afraid this is no laughing matter," he said, his fingers tugging the material loose and pulling the veil carefully from her crown.

Her head tilted back, resting against his shoulder. "I think I would have fainted away with embarrassment, had this been our first time together."

"Thankfully"—he kissed her shoulder—"we'll have no such problem. The only revival we will require will be in the form of sustenance between orgasms."

Her face flushed; she couldn't help that reaction. "Is that a promise?"

She stood with her shoulders pressed to his chest, her breath coming in pants, her body tingling with a sense of awareness that caused that familiar ache between her thighs.

"It is." He whispered the words against her neck. His lips slid a teasing path against the delicate skin.

Nick slid his hands over her shoulders, his touch firm, warm, seductive. She melted against him, like liquid clinging to a dry surface, wanting to mingle and become one. Her eyes closed as his touch overwhelmed her every sense. It truly was as if nothing but the two of the existed in the world.

Her head fell back onto his shoulder, and her breasts jutted out, though still bound by the heavy corset under her dress. She wanted him to hold her, touch her in more intimate places. She wanted to be claimed as only a husband could claim his wife. Skin to skin as their bodies crushed together in the throes of ecstasy.

Nick's mouth landed on the small bit of skin exposed at her shoulders. His teeth possessively scraped along the sensitive skin as his hands moved lower, tracing a hot and heavy path down her arms and over her stomach, skipping all the places that ached most for his touch.

He nipped her ear. "Lean forward on the bed, on your hands and knees."

She didn't argue or ask him to remove her clothes but complied eagerly. He liked this position most, and while she wanted to see him, she craved any touch he could offer her and willingly gave in to his command.

Skirts tossed up, the cool air in the room hit the back of her knees, making her shiver. Her breath stilled; her lungs froze in anticipation.

"I need your touch," she moaned, unable to remain silent.

"Soon." Nick grunted as he loosened the ties on her drawers and then yanked the material clear off her hips. Amelia bit her lip as Nick exposed her buttocks, his hand clasping each rounded globe with exploratory hands. He'd owned every part of her body, and she didn't deter him; she spread her knees wider, giving him free access to touch the places that she wanted to feel him most.

"I want you inside me, Nick." Never had she been so bold with her words. But the culmination of the day's events had her burning for his touch.

"Patience is a virtue I will have to better teach you."

His hand landed with a resounding smack on her rear.

"*Unf*" was all she got out as he rubbed away the sting, massaging her until she was pushing suggestively back into his hand, indicating what her body needed if he wouldn't listen to the pleas that fell past her lips. Patience was not a value she wanted to learn at a time like this.

"Despite what you think, you are a dreadful tease," she said.

"And you love how I make you feel."

It was hard to disagree with that. She loved it too.

She turned around on the bed, exposing her mons to Nick's ravenous gaze. He fell to his knees in front of her, his head disappearing beneath the swaths and layers of her wedding dress. The first touch of his mouth against that private place had her legs spreading more, inviting him closer.

A moan fell from her lips the moment his tongue slicked through her folds, tasting the swollen, needy flesh between her thighs. Married or not, she bit her tongue to keep from screaming out his name. What they did was between only them, though she didn't think she would be preaching that sentiment for long, because Nick liked and encouraged her to make noise when they were intimate.

Nick sucked the folds of vagina into his mouth, as though he was desperate to taste every private place he could reach with his tongue. The juices dripped from her core; her entrance was completely slicked and ready for the part of him she craved most, but she did not want him to stop the sweet torture of his mouth just yet.

The flat of his tongue moved around her clitoris; every swirl heightened the sensations washing through her body as she surrendered to his ministrations. Hands reaching above her head, she curled her hands and nails into the mattress, anchoring her and giving her a way to catapult her body into his at all the right moments.

Heart in her throat, breath abated, she rode toward the precipice of release, her pelvis thrashing forward, wanting him to thrust deeper as she clasped the counterpane as though her life depended upon it. She was torn between wanting to find her release and needing him to come over her as her hips rolled.

"I *need* you inside me." Her voice was husky, desperate. She didn't care how she sounded as long as the outcome was Nick claiming her as his wife.

Nick's fingers slammed deep inside her, eliciting another strangled whimper past her lips. His hand was relentless as he worked it in and out of her, his tongue lashing her swollen clitoris.

Amelia released her grip on the bed and grasped Nick's arms, trying to pull him onto her, to give herself a momentary break to at least catch her breath. To hold off.

It was all too much. Too fast. She wanted to draw this out. Make it last.

"Nick. Please…"

He bit the side of her thigh. It was enough to throw her over the cliff of ecstasy the second he sucked the folds of her sex into his mouth and flicked his tongue against her clitoris again. And then all that mattered was that moment of perfect bliss.

"Oh God, oh God. Nick, please." Her heart raced so hard and fast she could hear the thump, thump, thump of it in her ears. But Nick's mouth was unrelenting, and he ate at her until she thought she couldn't handle it a second longer. She twisted in his hold, needing to distance herself from the feel-good, too-good sensations washing through her but wanting more, all at the same time.

"I want you inside me." Her voice was growing thicker with need, louder in demand. "Oh God. I can't. I can't. I need more. I can't." She thrust toward his mouth, needing him harder and softer all at the same time.

When her voice was raw and hoarse from begging him to stop and continue, he released her. His body was suddenly absent, leaving her writhing on the bed, unable to do much more than attempt to catch her breath after the intensity of that orgasm. She felt cold without him and reached for him, wanting him back.

He only shook his head, though the set of his jaw and hooded gaze told her he was not unaffected by the image she made.

"Stand up, Amelia." He held his hand out, but it was far enough that she would have to stand from the bed.

She studied him through half-lidded eyes. What was he about tonight? In what adventures would they indulge?

Eager to find out, she grasped Nick's hand, slid to the edge of the bed, and stood as fast as her languorous body allowed. If there was one thing she'd learned about Nick in the time they'd been lovers, it was that a certain intensity and command was present in everything he did and said. She wanted to comply…be rewarded for her obedience.

Her eyes dropped to the obvious bulge in his beige doeskin trousers. She swallowed; her appetite had but one need of fulfillment, and that was to lay claim to him the way he'd done with her.

Nick clucked his tongue, drawing her eyes back up to his. The gray irises were but an eclipse behind his enlarged pupils. He pulled a handkerchief from the pocket of his waistcoat and wiped the evidence of what he'd just done from his short-clipped black beard. She should be embarrassed by such a brazen display of her desire coating him; instead, she was intrigued and reached a hand toward him, touching the row of buttons on his waistcoat, pushing them through the moorings as quickly as her fingers could manage.

When she finished that, her fingers trailed lower. She needed to touch the steely rod she craved more than any decent woman should.

"I have plans for you before you suck me off," he said, and that made her blush. He had such a dirty—albeit blunt—way with his words that she was always at a loss on how to respond.

"I don't think there's a better sight than my bride blushing when I've just attempted to suck you dry of the sweet honey you let down between your legs."

"Nick." When she said his name, it came out shaky and breathless. "I need you. I want to be together as man and wife."

He removed his waistcoat, letting it fall to the floor. Pulling his shirt free of his trousers, he yanked the billowy material over his head and tossed that aside next. Almost naked. And what a glorious man he was to look upon when he shed his clothes. His chest and abdomen were sculpted like an Adonis statue, every line chiseled with precision on his strong form.

"I'm feeling overdressed," she mused, her hands rubbing over her aching breasts that felt heavy and hot. She wanted to be touched by him with a desperation that had the power to steal her breath away.

"A problem easily fixed. Turn around."

She obeyed his command, anxious to be free of her dress. His hands were on her, smoothing over her shoulders and down the slope of her arms before curling around her waist. He was still teasing her. Taking his time.

"I haven't told you yet how beautiful you look all dressed in white."

"The dress is beautiful, the details exquisite. But I need you to take it off."

"There are no lengths I won't go to for you, Amelia."

She knew the truth of those words, she'd experienced just how far he would go to protect her, care for her…love her.

His hands dropped from her waist, only to start tugging at the strings that tied the outer layers of the dress together. As the cool air of the room caressed her bared shoulders, so too did Nick's lips in a tenderness that stole her breath all over again. It wasn't long before he had the majority of her clothes off. Though he had been careful with her dress, he did not remain so gentle with the underclothes. He tugged her chemise off her shoulders, where it remained, trapped by the corset yet to be removed.

"Just the sight of your bare shoulder has the ability to bring me to my knees. I want to worship ever part of you."

The rawness of his declaration, a small admission to his weakness toward her, made her knees weak. She wanted nothing other than to surrender to his every wish and let him do as he pleased.

"Nick. Please…make me yours."

"You are mine. Have I not demonstrated that night after night?"

"Yes, but not as your wife. Make me your wife in truth. Consummate our marriage."

"I have every intention."

Nick's hand cupped her mons and then rubbed her there, making her juices flow again. Amelia reached behind her and pressed her hand against his erection.

She squeezed him. "Take me."

Nick sucked her earlobe into his mouth, nibbling gently at the sensitive skin.

"You have the ability to make me lose all sense of direction." He spun her around so they faced each other. "Release me, if that's what you desire in this moment."

Amelia didn't take a moment to think otherwise; she pushed down his trousers as fast as her fingers could work on the ties and buttons, and then he was springing free, a heavy weight in her hand.

She licked her lips, looking down at the bead of pre-come that emitted from the tip. "Do you want me to suck it?"

He was backing her up even as she asked. "Later, yes. Right now, I want to fuck you until you don't care who hears your screams."

Her knees hit the back of the bed, and she was forced to lean back as Nick came over her. He had her by the hips and tossed her onto the mattress before pulling his trousers completely off.

Her gaze stuck on his cockstand before traveling upward over the roped ridges that carved the muscles on his stomach and all the way up to his chest. He was like a marble stature, gloriously beautiful and dangerous all at once.

Looking at him thus, she wanted to trace every line of sinew with her tongue. "You truly are a sight to behold."

He cocked one brow. "As are you, my lovely wife."

He knocked her knees wider apart and shoved her underclothes higher up her thighs, exposing her to his view.

As Amelia sat up, she hiked the material up to the lower edge of her corset, letting him get a good view of what she was offering him. She reached out to him and rubbed her hand through the spattering of hair on his chest. Her fingers circled his small tan areolas. Nick hissed in a breath and stared at her with nothing short of hunger in his gaze.

He took his time crawling over her body; his gaze flicked down to where she chewed on her lower lip. Amelia looked between their bodies, seeing all that virility hanging between them, teasing her. She swallowed back the desperation building in her. How could she show him patience when what she wanted was so near?

"Take me." Her voice wasn't her own; it was sultry, sexy, an erotic demand that he own her. "Take me...now."

He fisted his hand around the root of his cock and brought it to her entrance...torturously slow.

"I've waited for this all day," he said and then slammed deep inside her.

Amelia's back arched off the bed, her whole body opening like a flower to a bee, pulling him in deeper as her arms wrapped around his shoulders, and her pelvis tilted upward in supplication. The scruff of his beard abraded her neck, yet his lips were soft along her collarbone as he licked the sweat from her skin.

With one hand sinking into her hair at her nape to hold her tight, Nick pulled back only to thrust deeper. The air left her lungs with each slam of his body into hers. Neck arched, body bowed, she gave him free rein over their pleasure as he plowed into her until they could scarcely catch a breath between them.

Their teeth clanked as their tongues tangled in a kiss that consumed their cries of rapture. Amelia was lost to him. Lost to herself. All she knew, as they drew closer to their peak, was that when they were in each other's arms, everything was perfect and right between them.

Her nails carved crescent moons into the scarred flesh of his back. Nick's hand gripped the back of her head tighter, angling it just so that he could thrust his tongue as deep into her mouth as his cock plundered into her core. She was breathless and had no choice but to relinquish the last vestiges of control to him.

He let her go only to reach between their bodies and flick his thumb across her clitoris, his gaze rapt. He was waiting for her pleasure to rise before giving himself completely over to her. Waiting for her completion, and she wanted to give it to him but was locked in the perfectness of the moment.

Amelia strained toward that precipice of pleasure so profound she knew it would render her immobile for what remained of their afternoon. Still, she stretched closer to the bliss he so freely wanted her to have. He stared down at her, his lips red from their violent kisses in their attempt to devour each other. When her eyes caught on his sharp gaze, so filled with satiation and desire, she crashed through the barrier of her desire.

Amelia thrashed beneath him, her body desperate to move, to ride out the eroticism of the moment as he fucked her like a man bent on one end, now that she was taken care of. She fairly vibrated around him as he took her over and over again, her body unfurling in a need so great she thought she might die from the pleasure, and then he let go with a shout as he stilled inside her, his seed spilling hot and deep.

Their breaths mingled and teased as their kisses gentled, and he took the weight of his body on his arms, resting on either side of her.

Nick brushed the hair back from her forehead. "Are you all right?"

She nodded and gave him a sultry smile as she arched her back and stretched out like an indulgent cat beneath him. He palmed her thigh in languid strokes, just as reluctant to pull out of her as she was for him to break the perfect moment that had exploded between them.

Amelia trailed her index finger down the side of his jaw, scratching her nail through the neat beard she so loved on him and despised on all other men. The scruff added a certain animalistic quality to him.

She dipped her finger into his mouth, which he sucked and nibbled.

"I could perhaps agree to stay in bed for the rest of the day," she said.

The smile he wore made his expression go from intense to playful in a second. He flipped them around—she straddling his thighs; he still buried deep inside her and as firm as ever.

"That's a promise I can make," he said.

"I like when you make good on your promises."

"I always do."

"I know." Amelia lowered her mouth to his and let him distract her into the wee morning hours.

CHAPTER THREE

"Did you ever imagine you would marry?" Landon asked Nick as they stared down the ridge toward the manor house and the surrounding lands of Highgate.

"Not before Amelia came into my life."

"My sentiments exactly before I met Meredith."

Nick well recalled when Landon had met his wife and always had thought such a union so perfectly made would be impossible for him. How wrong he had been.

Nick turned his gaze up to the gray sky, hoping they wouldn't get caught in a downpour. Today he should feel on top of the world, having only the day before married the woman he loved, but something held him back from that idyllic feeling.

Shauley's waiting in the wings to cause more problems was likely part of the reason he felt reserved about his good luck. Here, he sat atop his horse, a man staring down at the land he'd wanted to possess for as long as he could remember. So why hadn't purchasing this land and the manor helped to bury his past as he thought it would?

The wind rolled around them, a reminder that nature was in control of unleashing a storm at any moment.

"So this is Caldon Manor," his friend mused. While they'd been here a week, and Landon had helped in the search effort for Amelia, they had not made their way out to the manor in the light of day to assess the property. Nick hadn't wanted to leave Amelia's side since the incident.

"Indeed. It is."

"You could have found a hundred different manor houses to convert. I daresay you could have found something in better shape too. Why this one?"

Was there a hint of skepticism in his friend's comment?

"I go back a long way with this property. It has…nostalgic value."

Landon cocked one eyebrow as he stared at Nick in disbelief. "Care to elaborate on this secret past of yours?"

"Not particularly." Nick squeezed his thighs around his mount, pushing the gelding closer to the old house. The sight of it still haunted him to this day. His past had started here, created the man he'd become, but his obsession in owning this house had nearly cost him Amelia. And that was unacceptable to him.

Landon wasn't far behind as Nick took his horse to a trot. They had a few hours to themselves before breakfast was served.

Caldon Manor loomed before them as they slowed their horses.

"It might be better to tear down the heap of rubble," Landon pointed out.

"True. But my sister has her sights set on fixing up this place to its former grandeur for her school."

And he had plans on making the town a better place while he was at it. There was so much hatred and darkness ingrained in the town that it practically seeped through his bones. That gloomy ugliness needed to change.

"How many acres surround this place?"

"Forty. It will be enough land to build houses for the families that don't take up residence in the strip of properties you are acquiring from this purchase."

Landon grunted as he led his horse toward the back of the property. Nick followed, looking at the house in a new light. He could scarcely believe it was his. Having purchased it with such ease made the whole ordeal seem anticlimactic to his goals.

They walked past a roughly made wooden fence that didn't look a day less than fifty years, surrounding an old vegetable patch full of weeds and rocks. The fence trailed farther, to the edge of the wood that lined the property. Nick's hand's tightened on the reins when he spied an old man hunched over in his dark brown robes, walking with a cane and carrying a basket laden with whatever he'd foraged for in the wood.

"It appears you have a neighbor," Landon said absently.

Nick didn't respond; he wasn't sure how to when he was staring at someone from his past, at one of the men who could have been his advocate instead of silently hanging back in the pews, letting evil happen in all parts of the school Nick had attended as a boy.

The old man was but a fraction of the man he'd once been, frail and weak as he leaned heavily upon his cane, and walking with a limp along an old worn-down path lined with stones. The old man hadn't noticed Landon or Nick as he walked deeper into the wood to whatever hellhole he called home these days.

Confront him, or let him be for now?

Nick dug his heels into the animal's sides. Realizing what he'd done, he eased up on the horse.

"It seems I do," he finally said. And he sure as hell couldn't go after the old man. Such forwardness would require revealing something of himself to Landon. The old monk was safe from Nick's wrath. Besides, that particular broken soul wasn't the sole person responsible for Nick's damaged past. That accomplishment was with the old vicar who headed up the all-boys school Nick attended when he was no more than eleven.

"I'll be sure to introduce myself another day," Nick said, realizing he was lost in his thoughts. He focused on the dilapidated manor house. The only way to describe it was broken. Something Nick could relate to within himself.

Landon didn't seem to care either way if they made friends with the locals this morning, so Nick further steered his friend away from thoughts of the monk.

"We've been gone too long. My new bride will wonder where I am."

"My wife as well." Landon patted the side of his horse and gave the house one last look.

"I've wanted this chunk of land for so long, it's odd that I don't feel an ounce of relief now that I own it."

"I find it's the things we are denied that we want most. And once we've succeeded in that goal, we wonder what our purpose was for wanting that end result so badly."

Nick felt no stirring of emotion when he studied the pitted, worn stone structure. Now that the first part of his goal had been obtained, his original goal seemed unfulfilled. The house was merely an object, not the source of his hatred toward this place. The vicar would be dealt with soon enough. Though Nick hoped he didn't feel the same lack of accomplishment after ruining what was left of the vicar's life.

"At any rate, you said it best. You have a new bride to get back to, and I have a wife to spoil," Landon said, drawing Nick's attention back to the here and now.

"Let's get back, then."

Landon rode up beside Nick and looked over his shoulder at Caldon Manor. "I still believe it would be better served razed. Less work to build something new."

Nick didn't look back at the old house; what he did know was that he wasn't so eager to erase any part of his past, and tearing the house down irrevocably seemed wrong. His past could not be wiped clean. The house would remain standing as a reminder that he had to keep fighting for all those children in future generations who were helpless to men like the vicar.

"I'm afraid Sera's heart is set on complete restoration. She wants a grand manor house for her school. She said she doesn't want the place to feel institutional. I agree that a house is more fitting for children." Nick had convinced her to take on the task of schoolmistress, with a grand manor as an enticement to the children's parents. "The way Sera's eyes lit up when I told her about this place…it's something I cannot take away from her."

He shouldn't lay his reasoning on his sister's shoulders, but his rationalization for everything was no one's business but his own.

"I'll never understand the logic of women." Landon shook his head.

Nick laughed.

Silence fell upon them for a spell, and all Nick could think was that he sure as hell couldn't figure out what went on in a woman's mind, but still, he wanted to get back to Amelia.

"It's the mystery that keeps us going back to them," Nick said, eager to be back in bed with his bride before breakfast could be served.

"Never did I hear truer words," his friend agreed.

With a challenging look at each other, they raced their horses back to the inn.

A few hours in her company would wipe away the memories that had invaded Nick's thoughts during his run with Landon. It wasn't just the mystery of how she made him feel that kept him coming back; it was her beauty, her kindness…her love.

Amelia had been awake for at least fifteen minutes but was too tired to even contemplate getting out of bed. She threw off her blanket to dispel the haze of warmth that grew increasingly overwhelming. The sun had only cracked through the curtains in their room, indicating just how early it was. Why was she even awake?

And where in the world could Nick have gone at this hour?

After the events of yesterday and their exertions late into the night, the thought of rising before the birds drew out a groan and had her hiding her head beneath a pillow to block out the morning light. She buried her head deeper into the down pillow, wishing sleep would drag her back under, but the longer she lay there without her husband, the odder she felt in not rising to greet the day and all it had to offer as a married woman.

Amelia couldn't hold back the smile at that thought.

Before she rose from the bed, the bedchamber door creaked open. She lifted the corner of the pillow with a yawn impossible to stifle.

"Goodness," she said, covering her mouth too late. "Good morning." She forced herself to sit up and took one look at the haunted look on Nick's face and pinched her lips shut.

So the honeymoon was over. He'd reverted back to his closed-off self.

What had changed between last night and this morning?

Had she slept through another of his nightmares? No, that simply wasn't possible.

"Nick?" Her voice was quiet, questioning.

"I need you." The starkness of his voice, the command in his declaration had her mouth snapping shut. She brushed her hand through the mess of curls that hung around her shoulders.

Nick stalked toward her, dropping his jacket to the floor without a care, unbuttoning his waistcoat and pulling his shirt over his head. He was divested from all his clothes before he even reached the bed.

"What has happened?" She knew she shouldn't ask, but the hope that he would share with her what troubled his thoughts came to the forefront and unleashed her tongue.

"Nothing that needs worrying."

Except for everything he always seemed to keep quiet about.

"We are man and wife," she said. "What do we have to hide from each other?"

"You have all of me."

Amelia placed her feet on the floor, spreading her knees wide to make room for him to stand between them. He leaned over her, his mouth hovering a few inches from her own.

"Do I?" she whispered.

"You do." He kissed her gently, tempting her to take more, and she did. "Your hunger for me makes me want to take you and fuck us both into sweet oblivion."

"Sweet platitudes will only get you so far," she teased him right back. Though hurt stabbed her heart at little that he kept secrets from her at all.

"Then we will worry about the state of us when we've hit that plateau."

She tried not to let the disappointment of his comment add to the insecurities she had, but it was no use. She felt further away from him than she had before they were married. And that didn't seem right. No. She knew, in her heart, that it wasn't right.

Needing to distract her thoughts, Amelia wrapped her hands around his arms and lowered her head in a different kind of surrender. When they made love, their connection seemed deeper.

While it might not be right in the grand scheme of their marriage, she couldn't refuse his need any more than she could deny her love for him and her willingness to do anything that might chase away his demons. Wasn't keeping her husband's troubles at bay part of holy matrimony?

She shoved her worries out of her mind and lifted enough from the bed that she could remove her chemise. She tossed it away and sat before her husband, naked as the day she was born.

Leaning back on her hands, she looked up at Nick with a wicked grin. "However shall we occupy ourselves, husband?"

His mouth was fierce as it landed upon hers, his lips melding at first and then stealing her breath away before she could temper the severity of his desire. Not that she wanted to mute his need. Not when she craved him in any way she could have him.

Did that make her a weak person? She couldn't say.

What mattered was that *he* needed her.

He'd come to her when his thoughts were troubled. He came to her when he didn't want to be around others. While all that should be good for something, it was hard to ignore the fact that he was still locking her out in some ways.

Nick couldn't say what had come over him the moment Amelia stripped away her chemise. The base desire that had been building inside him on the ride back to the inn, one that lent to his need for control, took over his thoughts.

It came down to how he felt when he was with her and the vivacity he always saw in his new bride. He wanted to take that precious quality into him and wash away everything that tainted the man he was.

Amelia was willing to hand over the reins whenever he asked, give him absolute control when that was the only thing that allowed him to put distance between the reality of now and the nightmares that took him over when his past reared its ugly head.

His lips tugged at hers, fierce, desperate. The taste and warmth of her mouth had his cock raging hard. He ripped his lips away from hers, wanting only to bury himself between her thighs, yet wanting to keep a modicum of control on his emotions.

When she looked at him with accepting blue eyes, there was no mistaking the ardor clouding them and mirroring how he felt.

He fisted his hand around the base of his rod, the tip already wet with pre-come, and brushed over her ruby-red, kiss-swollen lips. She flicked her tongue against the head, and a groan passed his lips. His need was so great he felt semen boiling up from his balls and ready to flood her mouth, and he pushed past the opening of her mouth, fucking it shallowly. She took him eagerly and sucked him in deeper. He nearly lost control then, but stilled and regained that perfect equilibrium that gave him power over his emotions and his body.

She was so goddamn perfect as she swallowed his cock with more vigor, as though this was the only thing she needed from him. That regained control was slipping from his grasp.

"Fuck," he muttered, voice hoarse as he pulled out of the sweet haven. "I won't last a minute if you keep taking me in your mouth."

Releasing his grip on his cockstand, he took Amelia's hand and guided her to her feet so they stood face-to-face. He caressed the side of her cheek, his cock flexing against her stomach, needing to be satiated, but he wasn't ready to finish this just yet; he was only getting started.

"There is nothing I wouldn't give to stay in this room, like this, for the rest of our days," he said, meaning every word.

That earned him a small, shy smile. "And what of your friends? Your family?"

"You are the most important person in my life and possess an uncanny ability to chase away the darkness inside me."

"Nick," she said breathlessly as she pressed the tip of her fingers against his lips. Right before his eyes, he watched her shed the daze of arousal.

Goddamn it. He shouldn't have said anything. He should have fucked her until they were both senseless. He pressed his forehead against hers and inhaled the fresh scent of lavender oil still permeating her skin from the bath they'd shared the night before.

"What happened this morning?" she asked.

"Nothing that can't be forgotten. I came back to lose myself in you. I like forgetting the larger world around us. I like it when the only worry we have is the two of us seeking mutual release."

Amelia's small, slender hands pressed against his chest, guiding him backward.

"Let me take care of you, then." Her voice was gentle. Soothing, even.

She led him to an oversized chair and gave him a little push when his calves brushed against the material of said chair, and he fell into the comfortable seat. Amelia looked down at his lap before meeting his gaze. When he reached for her waist to pull her closer, she smacked his hand away.

"Someone once told me I needed to learn the art of patience."

"I can't wait to have you, Amelia."

"I can promise the feeling is mutual. But I need to do this on my terms."

She lifted his hand, palm up, and placed it between her thighs. He nearly exploded when his fingers slicked through her cream; she was so ready for him. He buried his fingers deep, unable to hold himself back, even though she wanted to take control. She didn't pull away.

"Do you feel what you do to me?" she said.

"I want to suck the juices from your cunt."

She shook her head and placed one of her feet next to his thigh on the chair, opening herself to his ravenous gaze but still keeping herself far enough away that he couldn't do all that he wanted. Nick shoved two fingers deep into her sheath, pulled them out, and licked them off. Her breath hitched, and the cloud of desire ate up the blue of her irises once again.

Still…she waited.

Nick studied her carefully. "You're contemplating your next move."

"Perhaps." She nibbled on her lower lip, covering a grin that said he was exactly right.

"You are rethinking your strategy, because the thought of me licking that tight, throbbing clitoris has you dripping wet."

"And if it does?"

"Let me pleasure you."

She shook her head and lowered her hand between her thighs, opening the lips of her sex, like a clamshell ready to be devoured when she revealed the swollen pearl hidden inside.

His mouth watered, desperate for a taste.

"Touch yourself," she said, firmer, more sure of herself.

Nick caught her gaze. "You first."

She shook her head. "You forget who is in charge. I want you to stroke yourself, Nick." With her free hand she plucked at her nipple, further elongating the already firm peak.

His hands curled around the arms of the chair, and he started to lift from the seat. Amelia placed her foot square in the middle of his chest and pushed him back down.

"I asked you to touch yourself. I want to see how you rub your cock. How you pleasure yourself."

It wasn't the words that had his cockstand firm as ever and throbbing of its own accord; it was the fact that she blushed when she used the coarse words he had taught her. Catching her gaze, he fisted his hand around his erection and squeezed it.

"Your turn," he said.

Amelia dipped her fingers into her sheath, and Nick nearly came. He had to squeeze his cock so hard that he thought he might pass out. She left her fingers inside her and sucked in her bottom lip as she watched his hand slowly loosen.

"You're close," she observed.

There was no denying that truth. "Straddle my thighs, Amelia. I want to be inside you."

She pressed her knee down next to his thigh and climbed onto his lap. He released himself, his cock jutting against the wet folds of her sex as if his instrument was in control. She sank down on him, a sigh passing her lips as she did so. Amelia reached behind him and clutched her hands around the edge of the chair for purchase as she started moving over him.

Nick gripped her hips in his hands, guiding her, setting a pace that was both indulgent and frantic. Her breasts bounced in front of him, the nipples a strawberry pink and darkened at the hard tips.

"Fuck. You're so beautiful."

She thrust her breasts toward his face, and he didn't hesitate to suck one tip and then the next into his mouth, letting his teeth graze around the tight peaks as she rode him. Nick wrapped an arm around her back, curling his hand over her shoulder to slam her harder into his body as she lifted and sank down on him. His other squeezed her breast as he rolled the firm tip around in his mouth. Her hands were tight around his shoulders; her head thrown back as sounds of ecstasy fell past her lips without care or thought that they would be heard.

That he did that to her…

He released her breast with a suctioned pop and shouted something incoherent as his seed let loose in hot, heavy jets while her sheath clenched around him, like a fist fucking his cock.

She collapsed against him, the walls of her sex still flexing around him as she tried to get her breathing under control. Neither said anything as he lightly kissed the red marks he'd left on her pale skin from the scruff of his beard.

"I want nothing more than a repeat performance," he said.

She lifted her head from his shoulder, her hands cupping both sides of his face, her thumbs rubbing over his beard.

"I don't think my legs can move another inch."

Nick grabbed her thighs and rocked her along his semihard cock, already reawakening with desire.

She chuckled as she placed her arms loosely around his shoulders. She hadn't an inkling of just what she had done for him this morning.

He had come in here needing to forget the morning, the past that had been dredged up before he was ready to look it in the eye. And that had only been a small, unintentional glimpse he'd run across. What would he do when he truly had to face those demons once and for all?

"I've lost you to your thoughts again, Nick. Tell me what happened this morning."

He rubbed his hand along her thighs, and as much as he hated to end their morning interlude, he lifted her from his lap. She scooted off the chair and stood in front of him, unabashed and taunting him not to look.

He looked. The flush in her skin was fading and should be reawakened until it couldn't so easily abate. The ruby tips of her breasts beckoned him to suck. The dark thatch of hair covering her mons veneris…

With a sigh, he brushed his hair back from his forehead as he gave her a measured look.

"Intercourse will not deter this conversation," she said and crossed her arms, plumping up her breasts.

"Are you sure about that?"

"I want to help you, but I can't if you keep locking me out."

"It's not intentional."

He stood and walked over to the bell pull to call for a servant. He tossed her dressing gown toward her, and she caught it and slipped into the satin material. She didn't say anything. She was waiting for him to explain himself. Nick pulled on his trousers just as a soft knock landed on the door.

Nick opened the door for the housemaid. "Have the hip bath brought up and hot water. We'll need a breakfast tray as well."

"Yes, sir," she said.

Perhaps he could explain to Amelia why he hated Highgate so much. Give her an understanding of why this place had the ability to make him beastly.

"I thought we were going to attend breakfast with your friends." She was at his shoulder, her hand light against the scars that crisscrossed his back.

"We will make luncheon with them."

"What do you hope to accomplish, hiding away in our room?"

He turned toward her and lifted one of her hands to his mouth, pressing a kiss to the inside of her palm. "No one will think anything of it, Amelia. We are newly married. It's expected that we'll be insatiable for each other and antisocial."

"I will only agree if you'll talk to me about this morning."

There was no skirting around this issue, as she would have him figured out soon enough. Honesty might very well be his best defense. It wasn't that he wanted to lie to his new bride; he just wished he could forever keep her in the dark on his purpose for coming to Highgate.

"Landon and I rode out to the manor house. He hadn't had a proper look at it since arriving."

"I would have come with you, had I known," she said with a teasing lilt, trying to lighten the mood.

"You were sound asleep. And you need your rest for what I have planned for us."

He thumbed her chin and tilted her head back to give him easier access to press a kiss against her lips. He didn't linger; otherwise, they'd be lost in passion before either of them could stop. Not that that wasn't a preferable state of being to what he needed to tell her; the question was how much should he tell her?

"Nick…"

"When we were there, I saw someone I once knew. He was one of the teachers at the school I attended."

Her countenance grew fierce with a need to protect her husband. "Was he the one responsible for your scars?"

"No. He had the ability to stop it, but he didn't even try."

Amelia already knew a great deal more than he'd told another soul about his youth. It had been a short time in his life that he'd attended the all-boys school, but it had felt like a living hell he couldn't escape at the tender age of eleven.

"What did he say to you?"

"He didn't see me."

Amelia took his hand in both of hers and clasped it over her heart. He caressed the side of his other hand down her cheek.

"Perhaps you should confront him," she suggested.

"I intend to." While he planned to face the man responsible for the scars on his back, he hadn't expected the monk to still be here. Two demons he must destroy. He wasn't sure if that was luck or something to further torment his dreams.

A knock came at the door, interrupting their stolen moment of solitude. Nick and Amelia broke apart as a maid came in with a tray of food and the morning newspaper.

"Did you prearrange breakfast? I'm surprised they had something ready so quickly," Amelia said when the maid left.

He shook his head. "I wouldn't put it past the Lady Burley." He picked up an envelope tucked under the tray that was addressed to his wife.

"How odd," she said as she took the missive. His wife blushed as she read the contents.

"Are you going to tell me what is written?"

She blushed a darker shade of pink. "Merely that we should take all the time in the world since we are just married. But she did ask that we meet them for lunch."

Nick grinned. "What will you do with the knowledge that everyone knows why we want to stay in our rooms?"

She was nibbling on her bottom lip with indecision. Nick lifted the cover from the food, revealing a bowl of various berries, a dish of pastries, and another of bacon and sausage. "A breakfast fit for strenuous exercise."

"Nick." Amelia's voice was breathless.

He walked toward her, forcing her back to their bed. She didn't protest, and the look of hunger that ate up her gaze was exactly what he needed to see right now.

"There is no better way to spend our honeymoon."

"Don't couples generally travel to the Continent?"

He shook his head. "It's not about where we travel but spending as much time in delectable sin as we can manage."

He caressed her arm. Her whole body seemed to come alive at his touch. Amelia's eyes slipped halfway closed, and she swayed marginally closer to him. Her lips parted, and her nipples peaked hard beneath her peignoir.

"I do like the idea of remaining in bed all day," Amelia said. How was it that she could be sated by their lovemaking one moment and be desperate for his touch immediately afterward?

At least her husband had revealed what troubled him. A month ago, she wasn't so sure he would be so forthcoming with what bothered him. They had come so far.

Nick tugged the string that tied her robe in place. The delicate material gaped open, making her shiver. She was already slick between her thighs, from both their juices. Amelia took Nick's hand and placed it between her legs.

"You're not sore, are you?"

They had made love nonstop for nearly a day. That he was concerned and had asked had her smiling. "It's a good sore."

"Then we will play until the bath arrives." He tossed her down on the bed, coming over her but not entering her.

"I feel empty inside when you put me in this state."

"Perhaps this will help." He lowered his head to her breast and flicked his tongue against her sensitive nipple.

She arched her back, trying to get closer, begging him silently to take it into his mouth, hard and fast. He only pressed light kisses there.

Amelia lowered her hand and grasped his erection through his trousers. She wished more than ever that he was naked. That he was laying claim to her body and making her scream her surrender.

Nick grabbed her hand and held it above her head. "You were in charge once; it's my turn."

Amelia sucked in her lower lip. While it had felt good to have complete control over what they did, when Nick took charge, the things he showed her…taught her…

"What do you have in mind?" she asked.

He rubbed his thumb down the center of her lips; she stuck out the tip of her tongue, tasting the salt on his skin. His hand cupped her neck, massaging her as he rubbed his lips over hers. He didn't kiss her, didn't flick his tongue out, just rubbed his mouth back and forth; the heat of their breaths mingled and grew impatient with desire. Amelia curled her fingers around his arms, the corded muscle flexing beneath her hold.

A rap on the door pulled them apart. Nick was standing before she even processed the absence of his weight. He tugged her to her feet so she could fix her peignoir; she did so hastily, out of breath, out of sorts and in need of his touch.

Answering the door, Nick let the maid set up the bath. Two other maids carried in hot water and, before long, they were again alone.

"Now what?" she asked.

Hand around her nape, Nick pulled her closer, his lips once again a finger-width from hers. "Now we finish what we started."

He pulled off her nightclothes, leaving her panting and needy while she stood naked before him. It brought her great pleasure to see he was not unaffected, for he had to clench his jaw, and take in deep, even breaths.

"Why savor this?" she asked.

"Because I want to taste every part of you. Indulge both our senses."

"To forget?" she boldly asked.

He nodded. "I think we can both admit we like losing ourselves in each other."

Her lips quirked up in a smile. How right he was. She took a step toward him, closing the distance that separated them. Her breasts heaved up against his chest; her hand wrapped around his side and rested against his scars.

"Might I suggest we test the water before we eat?" Amelia kissed his chin.

Sweeping her right off her feet, Nick set her in the water, stripped out of his clothes, and followed her in. And as promised, they indulged in every sense imaginable.

Chapter Four

Nick took Amelia's arm and led her down to the dining room. It seemed odd that her nerves would strike her at such a time as this and that she felt panicked at the prospect of seeing his friends now. They hadn't attended their own wedding dinner, her feigning tiredness, which was the same excuse that had kept her from spending time with anyone for the past week, one she felt less guilty about using as the days passed. It seemed easier to hide in her room. It was easier to avoid everyone's questioning glances and speculating expressions altogether, but that was no longer an option.

She would hold her head up high.

She would be brave in the face of their missing adversary, Shauley. And she would thank everyone for the help they'd provided over the past week.

"Do you think your friends will be upset we didn't join them last night?"

Nick patted her hand like one might do with an aging grandmother. "Not at all."

He was pulling away from her emotionally. Putting a rift between them that she stupidly thought would be fixed once they married. How wrong she had been. Intimacy aside, it felt like they were growing farther apart. She needed to fix this. Now, all she needed to figure out was how. Hot, sultry nights didn't seem to be the end-all and be-all solution.

Amelia placed her gloved hand against her cheek. She was hot and positive she still blushed. A combination she was sure Lady Burley's *cosmetiques* could not fully mask.

"What is it?" Nick asked, his hand squeezing hers.

"I'm worried about what your friends will think of me. Of our actions," she whispered, not wanting anyone milling about the inn to hear what she had to say. Even though she was putting on a brave face, she still hated that anyone would think less of her.

"I can assure you that they have likely done the same."

"That doesn't help cool my embarrassment at being caught in your bed at all," she responded and was stopped from saying more when they opened the stained-glass double doors to a private dining room. The round table was almost as large as the room and covered in a cream-colored tablecloth. Dark wood paneling marched three quarters of the way up the walls, while the vaulted ceiling was painted hunter green. It was a cozy room that could be sectioned off for private functions.

Lord Burley stood on their arrival and came forward to take her hand. He kissed the back of it.

"A pleasure to see you both," Lord Burley said. Not a hint of censure in his tone.

"I have already arranged for tea and coffee to be brought in," Lady Burley said.

"I apologize for our tardiness," Amelia said shyly, though she forced herself to look Lady Burley in the eye without flinching in discomfort.

"I'd have been worried if you were more punctual." Lord Burley said this to Nick with a wink. Amelia could feel her face flushing anew.

"What are your plans today?" Lady Burley asked the men, obviously trying to change the topic.

"Huxley will be arriving later this afternoon," Nick responded. Huxley was Nick's right-hand man and once filled the role of secretary. Huxley took over some of Nick's business interests when Amelia had moved into the house and agreed to work as Nick's secretary.

"Has your sister already left?" Amelia asked Nick. She'd only had a glimpse of Sera at the wedding and had regretted not being able to spend time with her the day before.

"The school keeps her busy during the week. She said she could come back on Friday when her classes concluded, but I advised we'd be home by then."

This news surprised her. "I didn't think we would be leaving so soon."

"I have only a few things to take care of while we are here. Our business affairs should wrap up before week's end."

His explanation provided more questions than answers. Leaving in a few days was a surprise to her, since she hadn't been involved in anything he needed to do in Highgate. Something she would have to remedy immediately.

"What is there remaining for us to do?" She might be Nick's wife now, but that did not exclude her from acting as his secretary.

There was a moment of awkward silence that had Amelia looking around the table. Lord Burley held his wife's hand, focusing on the rings she wore, but Amelia saw the amused smirk on his face. Lady Burley was watching Amelia with rapt interest.

Amelia turned her focus to her husband, who was avoiding eye contact with her. A kitchen servant came in and set out the tea and coffee, her presence only extending the tension that was growing in the stuffy room.

Amelia didn't want to rudely depart now that they'd only just sat for luncheon. But she and Nick would discuss why he thought her role should change now that they were married. She would not be one of those women who gave up her pursuits because a man advised her of it. Unfortunately, now was not a good time for that conversation.

"I'm absolutely famished," Amelia said, steering the conversation in another direction.

"As am I," Lady Burley said, handing a teacup and saucer to Amelia and then making coffees for Nick and Lord Burley. "There are purportedly some beautiful trails for riding just beyond the village. I thought Amelia and I would take advantage of the scenery before we left Highgate."

Amelia opened her mouth to object but snapped it shut a moment later. Perhaps she did need time away from Nick. And a ride with Lady Burley sounded like the perfect distraction.

"I'll have Roberts ride with you," Lord Burley said. Roberts was Lord Burley's manservant, and Amelia had only seen him on two occasions and then, briefly.

"I'm sure we won't find any danger," Lady Burley said, a hint of objection in her tone.

"My lovely wife." Lord Burley brought his wife's hand to his mouth and kissed her knuckles. "You know I wouldn't dare have you riding in strange lands without aid at a stone's throw."

Amelia blushed and turned away from their display of affection. It was one thing to act such a way in the privacy of your room, but another thing entirely when the world around was your witness. She couldn't say she was embarrassed, more touched that they were so open with each other. Yet it wasn't a display she ever imagined between her and Nick.

"An afternoon ride sounds like a marvelous plan," Amelia agreed. "What time is Huxley scheduled to arrive, Nick? I would like to return before you conclude any business matters with the manor house."

She expected Nick to challenge her, but he only said, "You have until four. Should he arrive earlier, I promise to wait before conducting any discussions regarding the school."

Perhaps she had mistaken his meaning moments ago. Yes, she must have. She was overthinking everything. Expecting him to be a different man now that he had what he wanted. It was a silly notion but one derived, she supposed, from living with her brother for too long.

"Thank you," Amelia responded with a tight smile. She shouldn't have to thank him at all. It was her right to know what was happening, more so now that she was his wife.

She'd been such a fool to think marrying Nick would be cause alone to bring them closer; instead, it seemed as though a chasm had grown between them. That it was growing more as the days went by.

Lady Burley stood from the table and pulled on the cord to call for the kitchen servant. "I wouldn't want to waste the day indoors when there doesn't appear to be a raincloud in sight. Let us arrange for our lunch to be packed, Mrs. Riley."

Amelia set down her teacup that was still half full. "That sounds like a perfect plan. I can meet you at the stables in twenty minutes."

Amelia had to change into her riding habit. Thank goodness she'd packed one for this trip and only because Nick had advised they would be attending the manor house on horseback.

Both husbands stood as she and Lady Burley pushed away from the table; Nick assisted Amelia by sliding out her chair. How had they gone from intimately familiar to near strangers on the short walk from their room to the dining room? Perhaps Lady Burley would share some of the peculiarities of marriage with her on their afternoon ride.

Then again, maybe distance was all Nick and Amelia needed to better understand the new coldness that grew between them. They both needed time to adjust to the momentous changes that had happened in their lives over the past few weeks. It was no lie that everything had happened quickly. The thought that they were married, even now, was incomprehensible to the woman she'd been a few weeks ago.

Amelia kissed Nick's cheek. Though she didn't slip out of his grasp before he could take her hand to kiss the inside of her wrist. She pulled gently away, blushing something furious. It would make her monumentally and deliriously happy if she could stop blushing altogether.

"Good day to you, Lord Burley." Amelia looked back to her husband before they parted company. "I will see you later this afternoon."

Nick's gaze smoldered with something akin to desire. They'd just sated their appetites; surely she was reading his expression wrong. She couldn't help the shiver that chased through her veins. Then again, perhaps she was reading him correctly.

"Can I help you ready?" he asked, his voice low and tempting her to take up the offer.

She swallowed hard, her heart picking up in pace. That would not be a wise decision. Delectable, yes, but she had an appointment to keep with Lady Burley.

"I can manage," she said with a wink and turned from the room before she changed her mind—or Nick could convince her otherwise.

"Do you suppose they are still sitting in the dining room, wondering why they were left behind?" Amelia asked, drawing her horse to a stop at the top of a hill that overlooked the village behind them.

The day was typically autumn cool; the lands were a pleasurable sight, not as green as they would have been during the summer, but a rolling wave of grass that beckoned you to sit and stay a while.

"It's hard to say," Lady Burley replied. "I know they have other matters to discuss aside from the manor house. I believe they will parcel out the land between them, and they'll have to work through the paperwork and legalities of dividing those particular assets."

"I hope you don't mind if I'm forward, but Nick said Lord Murray disliked your husband and wouldn't allow the leases to be taken over by anyone else aside from Nick."

"Murray lets petty jealousy rule his actions. He only despises my husband because my husband is a better man."

Amelia quirked a brow. For some reason she didn't believe she was getting the full story.

"Truth be told, there is bad blood between them. I don't know the particulars, only that they once gambled together, and the game in question did not end well for Lord Murray."

"I imagine your husband came out ahead," Amelia said.

Lady Burley nodded. "Men are truly a peculiar sex."

They were, but Amelia had a different kind of experience— she was sure—than Lady Burley's and did not comment further.

Even though they were fairly close to London, the air was cleaner here, almost as if she were back at her countryside home in Berwick, minus the familiar tang of salt in the air that was present at her old home.

"The country suits you well," Lady Burley said. "You seem more at home here than you did at the dinner party at the Langtry."

"I could say the same for you. There's a certain freedom about the countryside and being away from the filth and bustle of a city that seems to never sleep."

"You are right. The slower pace is a good change," Lady Burley said with an amused expression.

"I will never forget the air of the Highlands. The freshness to it, the lick of the ocean playing at your taste buds. And the countryside...it's breathtaking when it's in full bloom of the warmest season," Amelia said. Lady Burley was, after all, lady of the manor from the far reaches of Scotland. She would understand why Amelia loved being away from the crowded city.

"I miss Scotland even now," she said. "But Landon insists on splitting our time with London; otherwise, business might lag."

There was a wistful longing in Lady Burley's tone.

"When did you marry? You seem as though you have known Lord Burley all your life."

"Goodness, we nearly have," Lady Burley mused. "We are coming up to three years."

"But you knew Lord Burley prior to your marriage?"

Lady Burley smiled. "We did."

"Does that make marriage easier?"

She wished someone could tell her whether or not things were supposed to change between her and Nick now that she was Mrs. Riley and not just his secretary, Miss Grant.

"My situation is hardly a good comparison to yours." Lady Burley's voice turned firm and serious. "I grew up in a neighboring estate to the Prices. In fact, my brothers and Landon were constant companions."

Lady Burley looked back at the manservant who was twenty paces behind them before she tied her reins around the saddle's pommel and slid off the horse as elegantly as Amelia had ever seen a lady do.

Amelia followed suit. Knowing she did not have the grace of Lady Burley, Amelia tossed her reins over the horse's mane and hopped down to the ground. Thank goodness she had chosen a horse that was no more than fourteen hands high, or her dismount would have not only been inelegant, but more painful, she was sure. She caught her balance easily and took the horse's reins in her hand so they could walk together.

"May I ask you something, Lady Burley?" Amelia was walking next to her newest friend.

"Anything," she said, her smile radiant as she stared back at Amelia. "Though I have to insist on your addressing me by my Christian name."

"I had forgotten."

"Forgiven, of course. I daresay you have good reason to have forgotten," Lady Burley teased.

Amelia blushed. Surely Lady Burley referred to Nick monopolizing the better portion of Amelia's time since yesterday in the only sense that newlyweds tended to acquaint themselves.

Lady Burley bumped into Amelia's shoulder. "I see you are still a blushing bride. I promise not to tell a soul how easy it is to make you flush."

"I had no idea such a thing would be so obvious."

"Of course it is. You would be ripe for nettling, should anyone find out, so your secret is safe with me." Meredith nudged her shoulder again and pulled away.

They stopped in the middle of a meadow with trees surrounding them on three sides. The manservant dismounted as Meredith walked over to her saddlebags and started pulling out the items for their afternoon picnic. Amelia fetched the blanket that was rolled up on the rump of her horse and found a spot to set it in the clearing.

The manservant assisted in fetching things from the saddlebags and putting them out on the blanket. He did not engage in any conversation with them and hardly looked their way. That action in and of itself was not strange for a servant; it was the uncanny way in which he kept glancing at their surroundings, as though waiting for something bad to happen. It was disconcerting being around him. And while Amelia always felt safe around Nick and Huxley, she didn't think this man would be looking out for her best interest.

Amelia rubbed her arms, feeling suddenly chilled. It had been less than a week since Shauley had kidnapped her, and she had to wonder where he'd gone to hide since then. Was he close? Had he left England? She wished she could forget about that man. Forget what he'd done to her. Only time would heal the fears that gripped her whenever she thought about Shauley.

Roberts stood next to the horses, feeding them pieces of apple he'd cut between bites for himself. There was something about the way he held himself; it was like a warning to others that at the drop of a hat, he would be ready for any sort of battle. He was almost like he had the same fighting instinct that Nick had.

"Does your husband's manservant always watch you from a distance?" Amelia asked.

Amelia tore her gaze away from the servant and sat on the blanket as Meredith opened up one of the two baskets that held their afternoon meal.

"Always. Landon is dreadfully distrustful to the world around us, and I suspect that Nick wouldn't have allowed you to come, had Roberts not been present."

"Because of the kidnapping."

"Among other things."

Lady Burley captured Amelia's undivided attention with that comment. "What other *things?*"

"Business matters." Lady Burley didn't enlighten her further. "I always knew the risk I was taking in marrying Landon. While he is a gentleman of the highest degree, he also accomplishes things that others of his rank find vulgar."

"When my father died, the taxes on the transfer of his properties were the last straw that broke my brother, Jeremy. Had my brother had money, I doubt he would have put it to good use, but his impoverished state is much like that of so many other lords, made worse by those who prefer to play life on a game of chance."

"I had no idea." Meredith seemed surprised by this revelation and gave Amelia a long look, as though she were measuring Amelia in a whole new light.

Amelia felt foolish for revealing so much...she had assumed Nick would have mentioned what had happened with her brother. And then she recalled all the other lost souls who lived under Nick's protection. Their secrets were their own; Nick had made that clear, as had the servants. It seemed hers were also of a private matter and no one's business, unless she chose to reveal the facts.

"Your husband has made a success of his lands," Amelia changed the topic, hoping Lady Burley would ask no questions about Amelia's past. "Is that not something others should want to emulate? It's admirable what he's accomplished."

"It truly is," Meredith said with a sigh. The love for her husband could not be feigned, and Amelia hoped that what she and Nick had was just as strong as what she saw in Lord and Lady Burley.

"But back to the topic at hand," Meredith turned her gaze toward the manservant again. "My husband has made plenty of enemies over the years. Not one of the aristocrats would care to emulate my husband; they want to crush him for not following the same path everyone else was forced to take by circumstance. Roberts is my husband's most trusted man and has stood by him through every threat that tried to tear apart what we have."

Amelia watched her new friend in silence; her sandwich lay untouched on her napkin. She and Meredith were more alike than she could have ever imagined or even thought possible.

"The same problem exists for Nick," Amelia admitted. Though people wanted to crush him for climbing out of poverty and making a success of himself, not for proving himself above the lords and ladies that ruled the upper echelon of society. "Yet my husband has no title. Only a name he has built with his own two hands." Literally. He had made the start of his fortune by fighting.

"Exactly my point. There are many people who would prefer both our husbands lived impoverished lives. That neither reached above or below their perceived worth."

"But this is the state of our lives, whether others agree it should be this way or not."

"Do you think your kidnapping happened by chance?" Lady Burley asked.

Amelia sputtered out a few nonanswers before giving up altogether. How was she supposed to respond without revealing more than she wanted?

"I believe Lord Murray sold these lands knowing your husband would eventually divvy up the properties. It's obvious Murray's man of affairs didn't think Nick deserving of the property."

While Lady Burley was referring to Shauley, Amelia doubted the woman knew the precise relationship between Shauley and Nick. Amelia felt as though Lady Burley was fishing for answers and for information Amelia wasn't willing to share of her husband's private affairs.

"I think there might be more to the story…" was all Amelia said.

"Oh, I know there is. And while I know you and I will make great friends, I need to know if you are the cause of all the problems Nick has had." Meredith bit into her sandwich.

Amelia's brows furrowed. "Why should you think that?"

"I know exactly from where you hail, Amelia. I could probably recite Debrett's backward."

As could Amelia. She was sure any lady born into a decent house had that ability, but it would be petty to argue that point.

"You already said Murray's man of affairs was unhappy with the transaction. It was his secretary who sought out an odd form of revenge against my husband."

"Then why would Murray's secretary kidnap you?"

"I think the answer is obvious." Amelia's frustration grew by the minute. "I will not feign innocence in my relationship with Nick prior to our marriage. Apparently, Mr. Shauley saw an opportunity to seek revenge against Nick and took it."

Amelia looked skyward; white cotton swabs of clouds moved with the breeze overhead. A loose curl at the side of her head tickled her cheek until she pushed it behind her ear and tucked it beneath her hat.

"I see now that your gesture of friendship is disingenuous." Amelia wanted to laugh. "Well played, Lady Burley. You had me yesterday, when you helped me prepare for my wedding."

"I do believe we can and will be friends. My concern is for my husband in the latest transaction, considering Mr. Shauley has disappeared."

Amelia gave Meredith a disbelieving look.

Meredith sighed and looked away. "I have lost people close to me. I am not willing to lose my husband."

"So you invited me here to better assure yourself that I wasn't a threat to your husband."

Lady Burley paused. "I suppose that's how it seems. But that was not my intention. I want to know more about this Mr. Shauley so I can ensure he is not a threat to us."

"How it seems?" Frustrated, Amelia set her sandwich down, her appetite diminished, her desire for company squashed. "I understand your reasoning. But that does not negate the fact that we are here under false pretenses. If you are so worried about Mr. Shauley, perhaps you should ask your husband where to focus your concerns."

Meredith twisted her hands in her lap. "He won't tell me anything."

"Perhaps that's for the better. I need a moment to think…alone."

Amelia stood, straightened her skirts, and walked toward the wood. Her intention was only to let the anger in her simmer and cool, nothing more. But she did not want to do that in Meredith's company.

"Wait," Lady Burley called after her before cursing something foul under her breath.

Damn the tears that fell as Amelia hit the tree line. At least no one was here to witness her humiliation and fault her for her naiveté. She of all people should know better than to trust another so easily.

When Meredith didn't seem inclined to follow her, and the manservant did no more than edge the horses closer to the woman for whom he was responsible, Amelia walked deeper into the wood for privacy. Really, it was so she could cry and pity herself alone. She would pull herself together in due time.

Amelia didn't know how long she walked—maybe for ten minutes but always within sight of the clearing beyond the wood. Checking her distance from the picnic area, she stumbled over an overturned, rotted-out tree stump. She wanted to laugh at the absurdity of the situation that had led to this very moment; instead, more tears snaked down the damp path on her cheeks. She was utterly ridiculous right now and had no one to blame but herself.

"Let me help you, miss," a craggy old voice said quite near to where she'd fallen. She almost screamed until she looked up into the face of a man who couldn't be a day younger than seventy.

"It's no bother, sir. I...I wasn't paying attention to my surroundings. The fault is completely my own." Amelia pushed herself to her feet and dusted off her skirts. While doing so, she got a better look at the old man. He appeared to be a monk, wearing a long brown robe, tied with a rope around his waist. A harmless figure, though she still remained wary.

Was this the man Nick had seen yesterday? She'd pictured someone much younger. More threatening and scary. She didn't feel an ounce of malice coming from the old man or the itching unease that had always enshrouded her when in Shauley's company.

"Are you from a local church?" she asked.

"Ah." He looked down at his clothing. "The church around these parts split into two sects of worshippers years ago. Half the men in cloth were asked to leave so long ago I barely remember some of their faces. I suppose that's the long way of my saying I do not belong to the local church. I am merely a man of God, living off the land as He sees fit."

Amelia looked back toward the company she had left. She couldn't see Meredith or Roberts now. Should she take a chance?

"Might I walk with you for a bit?" she asked. "I could use the company."

"A man my age has to keep up his constitution. A walk around the wood I can handle; it's enough for me to forage for some berries and vegetables the forest provides. I cannot walk much farther than I've already come." He laughed, the sound shortened by the fluid-filled cough of a man who had trouble breathing. Amelia pulled out her handkerchief and handed it to the old monk. "No, miss, I wouldn't want to ruin your fine cloth. But I could use your assistance to pick some more berries."

"Do you live far, sir?"

"It's just around the bend in that path." He turned and used his knotted wooden cane to point in the direction of his home.

"I would be delighted to help if you'll tell me which berries you want picked."

That earned her a smile, and for the next fifteen minutes, she helped fill his basket with enough berries to feed a whole household.

The crack of a branch behind them had Amelia spinning and nearly toppling over again on the uneven forest floor. It was Roberts. The panicked look on Lady Burley's face was one of worry as she rode close behind him. Had they been looking for her? She'd meant to stay within eyesight, considering everything that had happened; she must have lost track of them when conversing with the monk. Amelia acknowledged them with a dip of her head, feeling slightly guilty.

"We need to head back, Mrs. Riley. Looks as though a storm is washing through," Roberts said.

"Riley, you say," the old man said, staring at her with narrowed eyes and renewed interest. Did the name seem familiar to him?

Amelia smiled. "Newly married. My husband purchased Caldon Manor. We are here to assess the condition of the house, for we plan to restore it."

The monk grunted but didn't say anything. It became apparent that the old man did know her husband.

Amelia turned toward Roberts. "I would like to see this man home before we are on our way back to the village."

"It's no bother, Mrs. Riley," the monk said. "I can see to it myself. If you want to keep an old man company, I'm out here most days this time."

"I'm afraid I must insist." She wasn't sure why she needed to see where he lived, but it was important, even if only to advise her husband. "What kind of woman would I be if I left you now?"

Amelia took the basket from the monk. He didn't argue or make excuses. He walked next to her and led them toward his cabin. Roberts followed behind in his usual quiet manner and didn't ask her to leave again.

"Can I offer you and your companions some tea?" the monk asked.

"Oh, I wouldn't trouble you when you've already been wonderful company this afternoon. But I will look for you on the morrow, if that is all right with you."

"It is indeed, child. At my age I don't get around as often as I'd like to, and company is scarce in this part of the wood. Your smile and kindness have made the day brighter."

They wound their way over a worn path that had probably been carved and flattened over the years the monk had tread the grounds. There was a wild beauty about the place, unlike her home, where dense tree coverage was scarce; this place felt alive and ready to be explored.

"I didn't catch your name," she said.

"Where are my manners? Seems my mind forgets to do the obvious things at times. I'm John."

"And how shall I address you?"

"John will do well enough, madam. I'm a simple man with a simple name—no more, no less."

"You should know, John, that you make an excellent walking companion. My only regret is that I will be going back to London the day after tomorrow."

"Since Mr. Riley bought that old manor house, I imagine our paths will cross again in the near future." The tone of his voice never changed, so perhaps she'd read too much into the way he looked upon her when it was revealed she was married to Nick.

"They will indeed. And I look forward to those future walks."

A small cottage came into view after about five minutes. Smoke curled out of the chimneystack. The cabin was a single-story building but strong and sturdy, with a stone base and thatched roof.

"Do you live here on your own?"

"There is another from the old parish, but he can't get around like he used to. I fear his days are few and that he'll soon be gone from this world."

Amelia frowned. A sad situation for the other member of the parish, but not one she could assist in. "I'm sorry to hear that."

"It's God's way, madam."

A vegetable patch was dug up in four neat rows at the front. A fence had been built around the garden to keep out the larger animals that might scavenge through it. Bells were tied on poles, probably to keep out ravens and the like. Amelia set the basket on a workbench that was tucked up against the cabin.

"I will try to see you tomorrow, John. Perhaps my husband will join me and you can ask him all you like about Caldon Manor."

She wasn't sure Nick would appreciate what she'd done or if he'd be angry with her for approaching this man. He had forced her to seek out her own answers to the questions he created.

"Until we meet again, madam."

"Enjoy the rest of your day, John." With that, Amelia turned and walked past Roberts and toward Meredith, who happened to be holding out the reins of Amelia's bay horse.

"Upon consideration," Meredith said, "I seem to have been fairly rude. I sincerely apologize for my behavior. I only hope you can forgive my desire to protect my husband."

Roberts assisted Amelia in mounting her horse.

"You befriended me. Now I can't help but feel it was out of pity." Amelia clucked her tongue and turned her horse. She wanted to be back at the inn and out of Meredith's company. She did not hold a grudge toward the woman; quite the opposite, in fact. Had Amelia been in Meredith's position, she'd likely have done the same. More than anything right now, she wanted to reflect on her meeting with John and whether Nick would be angered by her boldness or thankful for the information she'd found out.

"Please forgive my earlier assumptions. Sometimes my mouth runs away from me. If you knew the hardships I had been through…had you been through them, you would want to protect your husband too."

"I do understand, but you still misguided and hurt me," Amelia said. "And you should never presume that your own hardships are more trying than another's."

Once their horses broke through the tree line, Amelia let hers run. She could hear the pound of hooves behind her following suit, but she paid them no mind. The wind tugged at her hat and loosened a few strands of hair, but it felt good to run free with her horse and she didn't stop until she was back in the courtyard of the inn. By that time, a light mist had started. The timing for their return was impeccable.

After dismounting, Amelia approached Meredith. If she didn't stand up for herself now, she might never do so. "I did not have a lot of friends when I was young, mostly because there were no other girls my age. The other reason was that my brother was a terrible man, and I didn't want him to do to others as he had done to me. I grew up being humiliated at my brother's whim. I will not suffer the same abuse because you fear the trouble I might bring to you and your husband."

"I did not mean—"

Amelia sighed.

"I know, and that is why I will eventually forgive you."

She hated to be cruel, but she was sick of being treated poorly. She handed off her horse to the stable hand and walked away before Meredith could try to *further explain* or make excuses for her behavior. Saying her piece had lifted a weight from her shoulders. It felt good. Actually, it felt fantastic. She didn't look back and was sure she wore a stupid grin on her face. She wished she'd been brave enough to stand up for herself while living under her brother's rule.

CHAPTER FIVE

On returning to her room, Amelia had enough time to lie down for a spell. She'd woken only fifteen minutes ago and decided it was time to make herself presentable before she went in search of her husband.

She rolled her new name around on her tongue. "Mrs. Riley...Mrs. Nick Riley."

Brushing her fingers through the remaining knots in her hair—the wind had done a great deal more damage than she'd thought—she twisted the brown tresses into a chignon and started to pin it in place. She needed something quick and simple so she wasn't late in meeting her husband and Huxley.

"Mrs. Nicholas Riley," she said to her reflection in the cheval mirror. It still didn't feel quite real, addressing herself as such, and it led to a certain amount of giddiness that she was even a married woman. And married to a man she loved.

"Only my mother ever called me Nicholas." Nick's rich baritone voice came from the door that adjoined their rooms. His presence startled her, making her jump a little on her chair.

Amelia's eyes searched for Nick's in the mirror. She was slightly embarrassed to be caught contemplating how she should be addressed aloud. However, the sensual rasp of his voice shot a twinge of awareness right to her core.

Well, that reaction was unexpected. But then, her good mood hadn't abated since standing up for herself.

"Has Huxley arrived?"

"He sent a note to say he was behind schedule. Stopped to help a carriage that got stuck in the mud."

Amelia focused on her hair again, thinking all sorts of wicked things they could do with their time. "What a shame. However will we occupy ourselves?" Swiveling around in her chair, she faced her husband.

Nick was without a shirt and his trousers rode low on his lean hips. The muscles on his chest and stomach flexed and rippled. Her cheeks flushed, and her nipples beaded tightly beneath her dress. A towel was tossed over his shoulder, and droplets of water held to his beard.

"So I should not call you Nicholas."

"My mother said it was a name that would allow people to take me seriously. A name that was strong, one to which others would listen and respect. It was also my father's name."

"Your mother named you well. And after a saint."

"I can promise you I'm no saint, love."

She laughed, her gaze traveling the length of his strong form. Not a saint, no, but certainly next to godliness…

Staring at him, half-dressed before her; she dreamt only of being in his arms. She wanted to forget that they had important matters to discuss.

Amelia stood. "Yet you will certainly have me screaming for the Lord before we leave this room."

Nick strode toward her. "Is that a promise?"

She sucked in her bottom lip, nodding, desperate for his touch but not willing to make the first move. Nick turned her to face the mirror again and took the hairpins that were in her hands to finish securing the decorative twist of her hair. When he was done, her head rolled back to rest in the crook of his shoulder.

"Didn't you need to discuss other business matters with Landon? We can't hide up here so soon after this morning. What will everyone think of us?"

"I don't give a damn what anyone thinks, Amelia. I will tell you a thousand times, there is no shame in wanting to spend a larger portion of our time together. I daresay it's expected." His hands rested on her shoulders, and he gave them a light squeeze.

"We cannot forget why we are in Highgate, Nick. And that is to conclude business matters with the manor house and the leases you acquired in the village."

"The house will be there later today. And tomorrow. And the week after that."

Nick kissed the top of her head before he turned her around in his arms. The crush of her breasts against his body sent a wave of awareness right down to her nether regions. She would never get her fill of Nick. He made her insatiable. He made her crave intimacy constantly. He made her want to lounge about all day in a make-believe world where only the two of them existed for nothing more than mutual pleasure.

She stared into his steady gray eyes. They were solely focused on her, his pupils enlarged. It was hard to miss the heavy, thick bulge of his penis that she could feel through all the layers of her skirts. She wrapped her arms around his shoulders and pressed harder against him, wishing she were underdressed too.

Nick didn't waste a moment in divesting her of some of her clothes. He started with the ties on her skirts and then removed her bodice with quick precision. She was down to her chemise in record time.

Her lips parted on a small huff of air. His mouth was just out of reach, their breaths mingling as the tension between them grew thicker. It was a tease, to see who could hold out longer. Her eyes were half-lidded; her tongue flicked out to taste her lips and suck in her lower one as she gazed at the sultry, sexy look Nick gave her.

Her body burned with need and her veins pumped liquid fire to every nerve ending in her body. She was hot with an excitement so profound that it accelerated every second she lay plastered against his skin.

"What time must we be downstairs?" she asked.

Nick walked them toward the wall he promised to take her against. "We will be late."

His comment had her blushing from her cheeks right down to her toes. She rubbed her aching, tight nipples over his chest with every step they took backward. The friction of their bodies didn't seem to affect only Amelia, for Nick's rapt gaze was smoldering with lust, and only a thin rim of gray remained around his pupils.

"You look at me like that for much longer, and I'm going to fuck you up against the wall, Amelia."

"Is that a promise?"

"Always," he said before slamming his mouth against hers, his tongue sweeping between her lips as though he were devouring her, one lick at a time. He possessed her mouth as surely as he owned and controlled her body. Their teeth clanked; their mouths sucked and drew hard on the other.

One of his hands skimmed possessively over her lower back. "The thought that I almost lost you is what makes me want to keep you locked away in this room forever. That you were lost to me for as long as you were…" His hand lowered more, squeezing one of her buttocks through her dress. "My need for you grows stronger every day."

She tilted her chin up, staring into his steady, strong gaze that had lost some of its playfulness. The resolve in those smoky depths was enough to cause her heart to skip a beat. "You saved me, Nick. No one else. Just you. And you haven't lost me. You won't. We were meant for each other. And now we are promised for a lifetime together."

"Still, I should never have let my guard down when I knew I was entering a hibernating bear's den with you at my side. I was tempting Shauley to do me damage. He knew, Amelia; he *knew* how to hurt me most."

"I'm safe now. And it was you who saved me. We can't predict what will happen in the future. Let us just take one step at a time."

Nick pulled her arms down from around his neck and lightly clasped her wrists between his hands. His thumbs stroked across the faded bruises from where she'd been bound and unable to protect herself when the detective and Shauley had kidnapped her.

"None of that matters now," she whispered, sliding her hands out of his grasp.

Amelia caressed the side of his bearded face. She loved how the scruff lightly abraded her skin, and she suddenly wanted it rubbing against her in wicked, sensual places. A half sigh, half moan fell past her lips.

"It will always matter. You are all that matters to me, Amelia."

Nick's fingers nudged her chin to the side, and he leaned closer so he could press his lips against her neck. He trailed those kisses along her throat, firing her pulse to a faster tempo. Amelia melted into his embrace, every soft contour and curve of her body molded against his immoveable but not unyielding frame.

She didn't want to go down to dinner any more than he did, and she surrendered to his touch, his slow seduction that ate away at the last of her resolve to meet their traveling companions.

"Nick," she whispered, her voice hoarse.

His fingers stretched over the other side of her neck. She leaned into his gentle touch, exposing her throat to the ministrations of his tongue and lips and teeth. Her hands threaded through his hair, tangling in the thick black strands, pulling him harder into her body. They were both breathing heavily, and a trickle of sweat beaded across her lower back beneath too many layers of fabric that hindered their progress.

Both of Nick's hands slid down the sides of her body, gathering the chemise at her thighs, holding the material there. Lost in each other's arms allowed them to forget all the terrible things that had happened. Allowed them to just *be*.

She could forget the niggling feelings she had, the questions that constantly bombarded her about her new husband.

She shouldn't be letting this happen. She should step away, tell him what she'd learned today, but she never felt so close to Nick as she did when they were intimate. And that might be selfish of her to want the feeling of perfect bliss that came from their lovemaking, but it also filled her heart to brimming when she had him all to herself like this. It made her feel whole.

When his hands reached the bottom trim of her corset, a yearning of fulfillment clouded every one of her senses.

"Can't wait," she uttered.

And Nick maneuvered her against the wall, lifting her in his arms so she could wrap her legs around his hips. He managed to work his trousers down his hips and free his cock, which stabbed into her sheath a moment later. They both groaned on being joined. Nick raised his hand and tore away the chemise where it covered the top swell of her breast. The very edge of her areola peaked out above the edge of her corset. Nick slipped his tongue between the material and her breast, rolling over her hard nipple and sucking above the binding that kept it hidden.

"Hold on," he growled against her wet nipple. And she did while he tore more of the material aside and lifted one breast above the corset.

Her hands were tangled so tightly in his hair, and her arms were so locked around his neck that she wasn't even sure how he worked in and out of her while doing all that. Their movements were shallow, jerky. Desperation stole over them both so that they moved faster, sweat slicking their skin where they were crushed together. Nick's hips rotated, his pelvis moving in a way that he hit her in just the right spot. And unbidden, and faster than ever, her body crested, the sensation flooded through her so fast she bit Nick's shoulder to keep from screaming with her release.

Nick's body was unrelenting and unforgiving then. He pounded into her so hard she was sure her back would have bruises where the bones of her corset pressed hard into her skin. He came shortly after her, his motions jerky with each pump of his seed inside her. He slowed, released her legs, and let her lower her feet to the floor.

Neither of them said anything for some minutes as they caught their breath, holding on to the moment as they stayed in the circle of each other's arms.

That was when reality came crashing to the fore. Her afternoon with Meredith, the falling out, the monk...

Her escape into the perfectness of intimacy was too short-lived for her liking.

She pushed against his chest, forcing him to back up a step and give her room. Her breath still came out in short pants, and her body trembled from the exertion and from the aftermath of pleasure. "I didn't mean for that to happen quite like that." But was that even the truth?

"I'm glad the afternoon started out on that high note." He pulled up his trousers, though he still looked deliciously disheveled. She wanted to run back into his arms and forget the world around them.

She gave Nick a small smile as she loosened her corset and walked past him. She had to change into a new chemise. "Joking aside, we do have important matters to discuss."

Nick lifted his head and gave her a measuring look. "Sounds ominous."

"First, we need to set clear boundaries. I agreed to live with you, learn your various businesses, and be your secretary. I agreed to those things long before I agreed to be your wife. The way you went on at lunch…I thought you meant to not include me anymore. And I won't have it."

"I didn't intend to cut you out. You are a part of my life. And I would trust no others to do what you do for me."

Nick walked away from her to pick up his shirt where it hung over a chair. He rolled his shoulders, drawing her attention to his scarred back. Every time she saw it, she felt a stab of pain overtake her. She wanted nothing more than to comfort him when he exposed that vulnerable part of himself to her, to hold him, care for him.

"Then why are you already cutting me out of the business with Caldon Manor?"

"Do you really need to ask that?"

"Frankly, I do. If you find my involvement important to your business, this is not something from which you can exclude me. I have a vested interest in seeing this particular venture succeed. But you have been more secretive than ever since we arrived. More secretive since you rescued me from the hands of two madmen."

"There are some things better left in the dark."

"There are not!" Her voice rose, her ire getting the better of her. "The less I know, the more danger I might be in. Don't you see that? Didn't my kidnapping prove that?"

Nick scratched his hand through his hair, mussing it more, his expression perplexed. Surely he knew he was losing this argument. "The less you know, the easier it is for me to protect you."

"Your logic is skewed. And it hurts me that you won't be completely forthcoming and honest with me, when the opposite is expected of me. When it comes to your sharing the full truth, you balk. You run. You avoid it at all cost…it's infuriating."

She forced herself to stand firm as he pulled on his shirt and faced her. She refused to be tossed aside from his businesses because she was relegated to the role of wife. Didn't he see that she needed to be important to him in all things? His secrets had the power to drive a wedge between them, and now they were locked forever in marriage. His running would make them both miserable in the long run.

She clenched her fists so hard her nails dug painfully into the palms of her hands.

"Do you regret your choice?" he asked, voice wavering as though he was afraid to know or, perhaps, more afraid of what her answer would be.

She hated the distance that separated them; it was like a chasm suddenly split into the ground, keeping them apart, but she could not go to him. She needed to stand her ground, be strong. "No. Never that. Never think that, Nick. I wouldn't have said yes, had I believed us wrong for each other. This was meant to be. We are meant to be together. I believe that with my whole heart and soul."

He approached her and slid his hand down the length of her arm. Their fingers entwined before he led her over to the edge of the bed. She didn't sit.

"What is it you need to know?" His gaze was steady and focused. She saw resolve there too.

"We should be direct and honest with each other, if nothing else," Amelia said. "That is not borne of becoming your wife but of mutual respect. Out of the love we share, don't you agree?"

"Yes." Nick enfolded one of her hands between his, not looking at her.

"Earlier, you said my attendance was not required when Huxley arrived."

"You're more than entitled to enjoy your time here and leave business matters to me after the week you have had."

"Coddling me will not help me heal from the ordeal with Mr. Shauley and the inspector."

"It's my job to protect you, Amelia. That was a promise I made to you, one I take earnestly. I failed you when Shauley slipped you out from right under my nose. If you think I can forgive myself for that, you don't know me as well as you believe."

Amelia rested her hand against his face. "And I have told you a hundred times that what happened, happened. It was no one's fault except those who intended to harm us." She skimmed her fingers over the lump that hadn't fully healed on his head. "You didn't escape unharmed either."

"I will heal. But the horrors they put you through, the things you had to endure…"

"You forget that I'm rather resilient. That I can bounce back to a state of sanity far quicker than most, thanks to my brother's cruelty. I will not let my fear rule me or sway my decisions. I thought you understood that."

"The failure I feel will not abate so easily."

"All the more reason to love you, Nick." She kissed him lightly on the lips, jerking back before it turned into another sweeping, heated moment they couldn't pull back from a second time. "Tell me something honestly."

He nodded.

"Do you expect me to be excluded from the business with Caldon Manor or just the unresolved issues with your past that constantly haunt you?"

A perplexed look stole over Nick's expression. Amelia couldn't believe how relieved she was to see that her question was unexpected.

"I trust very few people, Amelia. The last thing I want to do is bring someone else into our home. Or to have another deal with Caldon Manor. I have old business that I need to attend to. Something in which you do not need to be involved."

"What if I told you that you needed to involve me?"

"That I cannot allow." Nick traced his thumb over her chin. "I might have coddled you some this past week. I want you healed. I want Shauley taken care of so you never have to look over your shoulder for him. So you always feel safe. In time, the dust will settle, but for now, I want nothing more than to keep you safe."

"Are you so sure Mr. Shauley will come back into our lives?"

"I know he will."

"Why? What does he want from you, Nick?"

"Revenge."

"For what? You were youths when you last knew each other."

"What happened might have been a lifetime ago, but some things are hard to forget and to forgive. Besides," he said, his hand lowering to her shoulder, "Shauley can never show his face in England again without being arrested. That was all my doing, and he'll feel the need to repay me for the blemish I've exposed in his character."

Curling her arms around his shoulders, she went up on the tips of her toes and pressed her lips to his. "Then my hiding does nothing. He will either try to get at me again, or he won't. But his partner is dead, and I think he'll find another way to get at you than through me. If there is anything I learned of him, it's that he's smart. And pulling the same trick twice is too risky for the man, half crazed or not."

"It's still not a chance I want to take. You mean the world to me, and there is nothing to live for without you in my life."

"I refuse to be kept in hiding until Mr. Shauley is caught. It's no way to live, and you know that for the truth."

"It hasn't stopped me from trying."

He wrapped his arms tightly around her in a hug that didn't let up. She rested her cheek against his chest and inhaled the masculine amber scent of his cologne. It was comforting and arousing. She couldn't stop from splaying her hands over his chest.

"How was your afternoon with Meredith?" he asked.

She had hoped he wouldn't ask.

"She's very direct."

"I've only ever spent time with her in Landon's company. She is generally a woman of few words around me."

"Do you like her?"

"She is Landon's wife. I can't imagine his marrying someone dislikable."

"She loves him a great deal."

"I don't doubt it. They've known each other a long time, long before they were married."

"She thinks I will cause her husband problems, put him in danger."

Nick narrowed his eyes. "How so? If she should be worried for her husband, I'm the only person she needs look toward."

"My darling warrior and gallant knight." Amelia kissed him again, this time with more heat to it.

"I will speak to Landon."

"And tell him what?" Amelia walked away from him and took a seat on the chintz sofa that was adjacent to the fireplace in their room. "I adore that you are so fierce when you feel someone has offended me. I can handle Meredith."

"Now who's fierce?"

"You taught me well. And really, it doesn't matter, as we will be here another day at most and we must focus on more important matters."

"The school?"

The direction of his thoughts brought a smile to her face. "Yes, the school. I'm rather thrilled about the entire prospect. And I know it won't be completed for a couple of years yet, but it's something I'm so proud to be a part of."

"And I know you will do fabulous work together on this school, Amelia."

"Your sister too."

"She'll handle the school, the teachers, the enrollment. You have been involved from the start. And will be involved in every process to get it to a state where it can be used as a school."

She gave him a shy smile and turned her face away.

Nick came toward her and placed his finger on her chin to turn her gaze back on him. "Suddenly bashful, my blushing bride."

"You give me too much credit when I haven't done anything yet."

"You were part of the negotiations. That deserves credit, and I only give credit if it's due."

"Thank you." She took his hand in hers. As much as she'd like to laze about in their room in marital affairs, they had some errands they should attend to while they were in Highgate. "Can I ask a favor?"

"Anything."

"I met someone on my walk through the wood today. An elderly monk."

Nick pulled out of her hold so quickly from the sofa that she nearly toppled forward onto the floor before she caught herself.

"Nick?"

"Stay away from him." His response was firm…even angry.

Amelia followed him, because she was not letting him run away from something that clearly upset him. "You cannot simply order me about."

"Goddamn it all, Amelia. You don't know the trouble you have caused." He walked over to the bed and picked up his waistcoat, pulling it on in haste.

"Explain it to me instead of constantly running away from me, instead of ordering me to do something. Because I won't listen if I don't understand your concern."

"He's a danger to you, as surely as Shauley is."

"He's nearly seventy and hardly spry enough to cause me any harm."

"Yet he did nothing to save the boys in the school. He watched as each of us was violated. He watched." Nick smacked his hand down on the writing desk, punctuating each and every one of his angry words. "What more do you need to know so that you understand the kind of vile man he is?"

Nick paced away from her, picking up his jacket and slipping into his boots. Clearly agitated, he donned everything with quick efficiency.

"If you walk out that door, I will follow you." With a violence she'd never felt, she tried to dress as quickly as Nick had, but before she could button up her bodice, he was already reaching for the door. "Don't you dare leave like this, Nick!"

"It's for your own safety." He paused as though having second thoughts on leaving. She nearly released a breath of relief. "I'm sorry, Amelia. I have to do this on my own. If I could lock you in here, I would, but I'm giving you the opportunity to stay put and keep out of this."

Then he left.

Infuriated by the entire scene, she picked up her silver brush and threw it hard against the door. The hell he would leave her when she wanted nothing more than to help him, support him, and be there for him, as a wife should be.

The hell she would be told what to do when she could see how much the revelation of her meeting the monk tore up Nick inside.

Something thudded hard against the door a moment after Nick closed it behind him. He cringed internally. He would pay for this. Amelia would be livid, and she'd want answers when he came back—that's if she were even willing to talk to him at that point. Her anger wasn't what mattered right now. Her safety came above all else. And he'd be damned if that bloody monk would stick his greasy claws into Amelia. He had to put an end to both men's reigns of terror.

He told himself over and over again that it was better to deal with the monk immediately, but he'd waited. What he really wanted was to be back in London, not holding here in Highgate, letting his memories of this godforsaken place consume him. He wasn't sure how his hatred for this place would ever be overcome and wondered on his sanity for buying Caldon Manor.

Revenge.

Tying up loose ends.

Two very important things he needed in order to move on from the nightmares that haunted him.

The stable hand, a boy of ten with sandy blond hair, slender, and tall for his age, looked up from the saddle he was cleaning. "What may I get you, sir?"

"Same horse I had this morning, if you wouldn't mind."

The boy saddled up the horse, while Nick waited impatiently. He paced, unable to stand still and wait. Thoughts tumbled over in his head on what he would say to the old man he had recognized the other day. The old man Amelia had mentioned. Nick had brought her here, he reminded himself. There was always going to be the chance she'd meet the very people on whom Nick wanted revenge. There was always the likelihood that she would guess at his game and hate him for the ugliness the revenge created inside him.

"Here you are, sir."

The black beast from his morning ride bobbed his head as he walked toward Nick. Nick rubbed him between the eyes and rubbed his hand down his strong neck. He took up the reins and walked the animal from the stable.

Nick stopped and turned back. "I have one question," he called out to the boy.

"Yes, sir."

"Where does the monk live?"

The boy explained the location of a small cabin tucked along the boundaries of the wood—and far too close to Caldon Manor, as far as Nick was concerned.

It was time to face his demons.

He thanked the stable hand and mounted the beast that rode like the devil out of the inn's courtyard, almost as though he felt Nick's black mood and wanted to ride away from its darkness.

It didn't take Nick long to find the dirt road that led to the monk. As he cut through the border of the wood, the cabin came into view. A far cry from the grand residences the vicar and his followers had when the boy's school was underway. And fitting they should end up living like an old witch in the wood.

"Is someone home?" Nick called out in a booming voice that seemed to echo around the small clearing and front garden, loud enough to send nearby songbirds into flight.

Smoke billowed lazily from the chimney, so someone had to be here. Nick walked his horse around the perimeter of the house. He needed to make sure there were no traps, that no one lay in wait for Nick to be at a disadvantage so they could overtake him. There were no such things in play here, only his active imagination of the various scenarios that could unfold now that his enemy was within hand's reach.

"I've come to speak with the vicar," Nick said, still on his horse and standing near the door.

With one final glance around the clearing that was fast falling into dusk, Nick dismounted. He tied his horse to the fence that lined the garden and walked over to the front door.

The cottage was small, perhaps only one room, judging by the length of the walls on each side. The grounds were kept neat, with basic tools lined up against the house for gardening needs: a hoe, a shovel, and a rake. Ivy grew along the base but not up the side. Someone spent a great deal of time outdoors tending to this place. The walls were stone, the roof thatch but not waterlogged or weighed down with age, even after the showers that had washed through Highgate not an hour past.

Nick lifted his fist and pounded on the old wooden door. "Is there anyone home?" he asked again.

There was no response. He tried the lever to open it; surprisingly—or maybe not, considering the secluded location— it was open.

"I'm looking for someone who lives here," he said as he swung the door wide open. It creaked as it stalled and came to a stop.

The place was sparse—a table sat beside the hearth and was likely used for all meal making. A rocking chair and a leather chair resided in one corner of the room. A small table stood between them with a chess set atop it, pieces laid out midgame. There were two cots, telling Nick everything he needed to know about who resided here.

The vicar had to be nearby, his lackey following close behind. The coals in the hearth were still warm; hence, the light billowing of smoke coming out the chimney on his arrival. The wood was burned down to black, and dying before its cold end. Where could they have gone so late in the day? Surely they were abed by dark and up with the chickens he'd spotted in a rustic coop outside.

There was reading material and a Bible on the floor near one bed. A window ledge held a candle, the wax floating around it where it had melted down with use.

There wasn't much sense in sticking around, so he swung the door shut behind him and got back on his horse. A fruitless effort was something he hadn't thought would be his outcome today. Yet here he sat...motionless, without a thought on what to do next. Should he wait or return in the morning?

Amelia was likely livid with him, and she had every right to be, but she didn't understand what both these God-loving men were capable of doing. What they *had* been capable of doing. They were filled with evil. Darkness. It was a darkness that impenetrated him over the years, never letting go, feeding into his nightmares. He tore his gaze from the cabin.

Clucking his tongue, he rode his horse out of the clearing just as fast as he'd arrived. He would have to come back in the morning. If no one was here then, he'd figure out his next move at that point.

Damn it.

He didn't even know what the hell he planned to say to either man. Other than getting their confessions so they could be arrested, he had thought only of his revenge on the vicar to this date, not how he would actually carry it out, once given the chance.

His peripheral vision caught the tail of another horse riding a good quarter mile out from him. Nick slowed his gelding to see if he was being followed or if he'd just chanced across someone else in the wood. He wasn't one who believed in coincidences.

It could be that his eyes played tricks on him now that the sun barely kissed the sky and provided only enough light to give him direction back to the village, yet there wasn't enough light to make out the finer details of his surroundings.

He picked a slower pace, listening to the wood around him, trying to hear something different that might indicate he wasn't alone. There was nothing but the sounds he made in the coming dark of night.

He shook his head. Perhaps he was seeing things he wanted to see and not things that were actually there. The vicar would not outrun him or evade him for much longer. Of that much he was sure.

CHAPTER SIX

By the time Amelia dressed and made her way down to the inn's courtyard, she knew Nick had already gone. She probably could have followed on horseback, but she was out of practice and didn't trust herself to do so without injury.

She wasn't even sure where following him would get her. She was so spitting mad she was sure her temper was no better than that of a feral cat. There was nothing for it. She needed to walk off her anger. Walk off her frustration. Nick was always quick to cool his heels, and she should do the same.

Before she could make it too far from the courtyard, Huxley rode in next to a carriage—presumably the one that had gotten stuck in mud and that he'd lent a hand to free.

He was the last person she wanted to see right now.

"You have arrived earlier than we expected," she said, trying for a sunny disposition but knowing she failed as her smile felt feigned even to her.

"Rode like the wind, Mrs. Riley."

"It's through no fault of your own, Huxley. I wasn't sure we would even see you this night."

"Here now," he said in his gruff manner.

"I'm sorry you couldn't attend the ceremony. You are important to us both, and it would have meant a lot to have you there." Especially me, she wanted to say, for he was the first person to reluctantly befriend her, but befriend her he had.

Huxley's expression warmed, but she doubted anyone would see the nuance in the way his eyes softened slightly. "Wished to have been here, I did."

"Your trip here was longer than anticipated. Why don't you set yourself up in your room, rest a while, and take your evening meal? I have some errands to attend." Errands? Was that truly all she could come up with? Hopefully Huxley didn't read through her lie.

"I'll see you later." Huxley doffed his hat before steering his horse toward the stables.

She left the courtyard without so much as a glance backward. If she waited, it would become obvious that Nick was nowhere about. That she was alone, and that would prompt Huxley to follow and keep his ever-watchful eye on her. What she needed was time alone with her thoughts, and she could not do that in a room she shared with her husband, where his things were all about, mixed with hers.

That she had presumed marriage to be the solution to their problems forced a nervous laugh past her lips.

If there was one thing she had learned from the past day, it was that marriage was hard. Relationships were hard.

Fundamentally, she'd known marrying Nick was not the magical answer to solving the issues that lay unresolved between them. If marriage were easy, people would rush into it without a second thought, as the benefits and intimacy were enough to entice many, she was sure.

Her problem lay in the fact that Nick refused to share parts of himself he deemed too frightening or too much for her to handle. How was he to determine that?

Then there was the fact that he would close himself off when his dreams bothered him, when he woke in a terror in the middle of the night, ready to strangle her—though that had only happened once. Shouldn't he try to explain why he acted the way he did? Give her the details of his dreams so that she could help him when they came to him the next time? Since they'd been in Highgate, the frequency of his dreams had increased. They seemed to come every other day, and only because he was forced to sleep at some point and not pace their room all night long, trying to avoid whatever was haunting him. He thought she didn't know, but she did. She knew well that he was tormented by this place and had known it since they had arrived in the quaint village.

She felt helpless in so many ways. Partly because she didn't know how to assist her husband at crucial points and because he was too stubborn to share the content of his nightmares.

Who knew men could be so insufferable when something wasn't going their way?

And while that might not be a fair way of viewing Nick's…circumstance, how could she see it any other way when his only reaction was to shut himself off from her? He resorted to locking her out of his true feelings and keeping her from his real thoughts.

There was nothing he didn't know about her.

Absolutely nothing. And that was what infuriated her most. She inhaled deeply and tipped her head back to look at the stars twinkling to life. It was peaceful out here. And it chased away the negative thoughts that had taken hold of her mind.

It was coming up to dark, and she'd wandered pretty far from the inn. She turned back toward the village, looking at the lights that sparked to life along the main street and guided her way.

Pulling her shawl tighter around her shoulders to keep the chill of the night from sinking into her bones, she enjoyed the solitude for a moment and looked up at the stars one last time. A night under the stars…she should drag Nick out here; he'd appreciate the calm of this place.

It was peaceful here, and she liked it a great deal more than she liked the bustle and noise of London. Her country roots were starting to shine through in this beautiful countryside. But her place was by her husband's side. Wherever he was, she knew she had to be. Truth be told, she'd follow him to the ends of the world, even when he was acting insufferable…because she loved him.

With a newfound resolve that surprised her, she knew she would figure out what made him tick. And she'd figure out a way to get him to open up to her. *Patience*, she counseled herself, and laughed, as that was what Nick always said when he was teasing her.

She exhaled a sigh and headed in the direction of the inn. It wasn't long before hooves clomped along the ground behind her in a steady tempo.

With a smile on her face, she turned, expecting to see Nick and hoping to find him in a better mood. What she got was something unexpected and too frightening for words. She couldn't be sure he saw her or even knew who she was in the twilight of evening; all she knew was that Nick's worries were intuitively correct.

Amelia picked up her skirts without a second thought and ran as fast as her heeled boots would carry her. She couldn't be more than quarter mile from the inn. But damn it, she could not outrun a horse.

A sob escaped her throat, and she stumbled in her path before righting herself and running again. Her lungs burned for air and she grew lightheaded the more she exerted herself.

Her shawl loosened, and she lost it at some point. She didn't dare stop to find it. She just pushed herself harder to move her legs faster, searching the village for another person walking about, searching for anyone who might save her from the monster riding on her heels. She could scream, but it would not help her if there was no one to come to her aid.

"Hold!" Shauley yelled in a timbre that commanded her to stop.

Amelia ignored him. She knew without a doubt that her life depended upon her reaching the village, which seemed so close before, but now, in the reality of this situation, was too far for comfort.

Why hadn't she heeded Nick's warnings? Why had she been so bloody stubborn?

"Hold, I say." Shauley was closer now; she could almost feel his breath on the back of her neck as fear crawled over her skin.

The scenario reminded her of when she'd been his captive, imprisoned to his whims. All the emotions that had trapped her then came to the fore. Helpless, afraid. Unable to save herself. She swore to herself that she would heed every one of Nick's warnings if she got out of this situation. She would do whatever he asked, no matter how much it angered her.

She let out a yelp as Shauley grabbed the back of her dress and hauled her up into the saddle of his horse. She struggled against him, trying to shoot out her fists, her elbows, her knees. Anything that would get her out of his grasp.

The horse halted suddenly, and the black creature reared up on its back legs. That's when Amelia completely let go, hoping she'd fall. She'd take her chances if it meant getting out of Shauley's clutches. As horrible a thought as it was, she'd rather be dead than taken by him again.

"Damn it, woman. If you'd hold still, I'll settle us down."

"Let me go!"

She gave him a good jab in the ribs with her elbow. The air whooshed out of his lungs.

"Goddamn it. Sit still, and I'll release you."

"You expect me to believe you?" She renewed her struggle, but he only captured her arms—which belied the true strength of his slender frame—and managed to get one of his legs over both of hers.

With one hand, he grasped her neck, holding her tight and narrowing the path of her breathing. "I told you to stop."

"Let go." Her voice was strangled, breathless. She felt faint and focused on just breathing. She would not be able to defend herself if she lost consciousness.

"I'm going to let you go slowly. And you are going to behave."

Her eyes started to drift shut, and black dots filled her vision.

When her arms went limp and lost all fight, he released her. He dropped her to the ground, and she landed with a heavy thud and a stab of pain through her hip and side.

"So much better now that you're cooperating." His voice was sinister, evil.

She didn't answer him, not that she had a voice to do so. She breathed deeply, trying to gather her wits and find the strength she would need to run again. Because she refused to sit in the grass, helpless.

"Imagine my luck finding you wandering about the lovely countryside, alone. Where is your other half?" Shauley asked, leaning forward on his horse so that the heat of his rancid breath washed over her.

She tucked her leg under her and hissed in a pained breath. "What do you want?" Her voice was broken and raspy.

"Now, that is the question of the hour. There are so many things I require and so little time to obtain them. Believe it or not, I intend you no harm."

She didn't believe him. How could she?

"Then let me go." Amelia wiped the back of her hand over her mouth, the cooper taste in her mouth indicated that it bled.

"Not yet," he said, as if they had all the time in the world. "I want to keep you a while longer."

Like she was some sort of pet? She bit her lip to keep it from trembling.

"You will not keep me here." Amelia snapped her mouth shut. She probably shouldn't have said that. She knew, fundamentally, that Shauley walked a fine line between right and wrong in this moment.

"I'll just run you over with my horse, should you try to escape me again. I can't recommend that form of death…quite painful."

She swallowed against the nerves building in her, making her afraid to defend herself. She would not be a helpless victim of Shauley's ever again, or any man who thought he could cause her harm.

"What am I supposed to do to help you?" Her voice was low, defeated. She could not let him win so easily.

"Just provide your assistance."

She nearly laughed but tamped down on the urge. He couldn't be serious. Why wasn't he stark, raving mad and dragging her off to the nearest hiding hole to torture her?

"I will not help you."

"It comes with an exchange for your husband's safety."

And why was Shauley so sure he could hurt her husband?

"How chivalrous," she hissed as she tested her leg, which seemed to be moving well enough.

"Hardly. I need no reason for your husband to come looking for me. I have something I have to take care of, and he's getting in the way."

Amelia pushed to her feet, feeling so much pain in her hip she nearly collapsed under her own weight. She took in a deep breath and focused on holding herself up. She must remain strong. If Shauley hadn't hurt her yet, perhaps he wouldn't. She nearly scoffed at her own stupidity. The pain in her hip had gotten to her head already.

"How do you go from kidnapping me, threatening my life, to wanting to have a civil conversation?"

"Recent circumstances have forced me to reevaluate my goals." This was the calm, intelligent secretary to whom she'd first been introduced speaking to her, not the evil, sinister man who had kidnapped and then hurt her before Nick had saved her.

"Might I ask what that goal is? You had a decent life as Lord Murray's secretary. You threw it all away to get revenge on my husband."

Shauley made a gruff noise in the back of his throat. "It all had a purpose. I had plans in place before your husband ruined it for me."

Amelia tested her foot and nearly toppled over when she attempted to take a step back. She wobbled in place. She could not risk being taken by this madman again. She had to get her body moving, get away from this place and to somewhere safe. But how, when he'd already pointed out his horse was far faster than she? She believed him when she said he would run her down with the beast he rode upon.

"There is a bounty on you," she reminded him, hoping it would make him think twice about being here, make him seek shelter hopefully without her in tow.

"One your husband so graciously put out for my capture. You'll find I'm a rather industrious man and not easily caught."

None of this conversation felt real. Why wasn't Shauley trying to hurt her? He seemed perfectly normal.

"Are you telling me you have been hiding close to the village, waiting for the perfect moment to capture me again?"

"I was taken by surprise, finding you on the road. Taking you is too much a risk. I know that now."

"Because Inspector Laurie is dead?"

She was amazed at how calm she sounded. On the inside she was ten kinds of horrified to be having a conversation with this sick man. He was too calm and collected right now. That frightened her more than his irrational side with which she'd been previously acquainted.

Something dark flickered in Shauley's eyes. Amelia braced herself and took another step back from him.

"Yes, the good inspector. I almost miss his company."

"No good comes of you being here. Let me go."

"You are free to go, but I want you to do one thing for me."

She held her head up high and gave him a cross look. Showing him just how much she feared him would give him the upper hand.

"I want Nick gone from Highgate," Shauley said simply. "He is here to accomplish something that gets in the way of my plans."

"You will have to be more specific." She was digging for information, and Shauley likely knew it.

He tsked. "Nick was always here for one purpose…"

"To build the school." She supplied the words, knowing that wasn't the answer but not knowing how to get the information she wanted out of Shauley.

Shauley laughed. "Is that what you believe?"

"It's the truth." She would not give Shauley more information than that. While that might not have been Nick's original intention, according to her captor, it was certainly Nick's purpose now.

Shauley dismounted and came toward her, grabbing her arms and pushing his face into hers. Amelia couldn't move fast enough to get away, so she held still and didn't make a sound.

"I see why he likes you so much." Shauley ran his leather-gloved hand down one of her cheeks.

She jerked her head away from him. Everything about him made her skin crawl to get away.

"You're a feisty little thing. Which is no surprise, considering the type of man your brother was." There was an undertone of treat to his words.

"Let me go." She all but spat the words.

Amelia needed out of his clutches. If she at least felt as if she were in control of the situation, she could handle this odd conversation she was having with Shauley. The ideal solution would be for someone to come upon them, but that didn't seem likely, considering her luck so far today.

He released her. Just like that. She blinked rapidly, not sure how to handle the change in power. Though she knew she had no chance of outrunning him.

Not willing to test her boundaries yet, she raised her hands in surrender.

"Don't test my patience," he said, his finger pointed at her like one might point a finger to scold a child.

"I don't understand what it is you want from me."

"You and Nick are going back to London. Tomorrow, I think."

There was no need to mention they planned on leaving in two days' time. "And what shall I say to him?"

"I don't care how you get him to leave, as long as you accomplish that outcome."

That they were having this conversation at all left her feeling shaken. Disturbed. She wrapped her arms around her shoulders, wishing she had her shawl to keep the cool night air at a distance.

"He seeks a mutual acquaintance," Shauley said, revealing nothing more than she already knew. "I'm afraid he's interfering with my plans."

"And should he refuse to leave until he seeks out this mutual acquaintance of yours?"

"If he gets in my way, I'll end him the same way he put a stop to Laurie."

The inspector who had helped Shauley kidnap her had been shot fatally through the chest. Nick seemed to have had no reservations about killing the man, but it had been him or them. A shiver of warning chilled Amelia right down to her bones.

"Tell me what you both want from this man." She didn't know if she would eventually push him over the edge and reveal this man's violent and crazed side again, but she needed to know, much like the deeply maudlin needed their next tincture of laudanum.

"Curious little kitten, aren't you?"

"You forget that it is you asking for my help," she challenged him, not sure if she would regret letting her tongue run away from her.

How could she pry more information out of him? They weren't long together if he continued to walk toward the village. Hopefully, she wasn't being fooled that he would let her go free.

"I know they were both part of the school. What do you want with them?"

Shauley's gaze was hard to decipher, though he seemed intrigued by her questions. "So he's told you some of it. Interesting."

For this game, it might be wise to pretend to know more than she did. Information tended to slip when one thought the other party was already in on the secret.

"Which one of them whipped him?" she asked, biting her tongue too late.

Shauley chuckled, the sound dark and sickening. Amelia did not lose sight of her goal; she needed to get to safety, and that safety was less than a quarter of a mile away.

"They all whipped us into compliance, my innocent lady. If you think it was only the heavy hand of one to make his back bleed, you truly don't understand the gravity of the situation we were in as youths."

"I understand it well enough."

Shauley whipped around and grabbed her wrist to the point of pain. He pulled her close; his face was within inches of hers again. She caught a glimpse of the monster he was, his calm expression slipping away to reveal something more sinister and calculating beneath.

She hoped she hadn't lost what advantage she'd gained and cursed her stupidity in questioning him at all.

"You can never understand it unless you lived through it. Nick and I were no strangers to the way of some men and the harshness they could deliver."

She didn't reveal that she knew what was expected of the boys, that they were overpowered, that they were made to do things that might have them question their worth, their very strength as men.

She twisted her hand, but Shauley held fast.

"What purpose do you have with the vicar? You said you spent most of your life here, growing up and living in this place. Did you never seek out the vicar before now? Or is your revenge rooted in the fact that Nick desires to see justice against that man?"

"I should have given you more credit. It seems you've pieced enough of our past together to make you all too knowing."

She didn't need Shauley to fill in the rest of the situation. She knew why Nick was here. His purpose with the vicar was the only thing she hadn't figured out. And *that* she would find out directly from the source.

If she made it back to the inn without harm.

"Did you know my brother?" she asked, needing to understand how her brother's murder fit in to all of this. "Before you ordered his death, did you know him at all?"

"That man was the devil incarnate. My treatment of you was far grander than his treatment of women altogether."

That was likely true, but she did not confirm her belief in that. One monster was not better than another. Shauley was no hero, even if he thought himself to be so.

"Did you kill him?"

"In a manner of speaking."

"I lived with him for the majority of my life. There is nothing you can say that will shock my sensibilities." She didn't know why she'd given Shauley that much information.

"You're a cheeky lass, aren't you?"

"And you are a scoundrel of the worst sort. Nick said you stayed on at the school after he left. Does that make you the same kind of man as the vicar? Did the vicar mold you into an image of himself?"

Shauley made a noise of disgust in the back of his throat. His hand whipped out so fast she didn't see it coming, even though she'd been nettling the viper all along. His grip was firm, harsh, and deadly as it wrapped around her throat for a second time that night.

Amelia's stomach was in her throat when he turned her around, her back to his chest, her body completely in his hold. It was full dark now, and she could only just make out the lights in the village houses.

"I could kill you now," he whispered in her ear, even though no one could hear them. The threat was very real, and Amelia wanted to kick herself for being so bold. Freedom had been close, and she'd thrown it away in anger and frustration.

She whimpered. She could not stop the helpless sound from bubbling up in her throat.

"Your only task is to ensure Nick leaves Highgate. I wouldn't want to have to find you again. I promise, the next time we meet, I won't be so forgiving and lenient. Do you understand what I'm saying?"

She nodded, since she could not speak.

He released her just as suddenly as he'd caught her. She gasped for a full breath and fell to her hands and knees in the grass. Her hand covered her throat, and she carefully took in deep breaths, trying to steady her nerves.

When she felt steady enough, she looked up at Shauley. "What do you plan for the vicar?"

"Curiosity eventually killed that cat," he responded as he swung up onto his horse. "Do not tell Nick of our meeting."

She would make no promises, though she did nod, not wanting to incite his anger further, not when freedom was within her grasp. But could she tell Nick of this run-in with Shauley? A part of her knew it would be better to just escape this place and head back to London; the logical and rational side of her said she should tell her husband so that he could take appropriate steps to capture Shauley with the authorities. But what if that should cause her husband injury, or worse, death?

"We all live for a purpose, Mrs. Riley."

"And when that purpose is realized?"

"That depends on the purpose."

"What do you plan to do to the vicar?" she repeated.

"Watch him die, of course," he said, as though she should have guessed that all along.

Amelia took a step back, her reaction eliciting a stream of laughter from Shauley. Her hip still hurt from her fall, and she doubted she could run far, so she held steady.

Shauley tilted his head to the side, as though he heard something she did not. His focus was sharp when he caught her eyes. "I counsel you once more against telling Nick we had this conversation."

"We are in agreement on that."

"I won't take kindly to finding you here alone on the morrow." Shauley dug his heels into his horse's side and was off into the night as though he had never been there.

Worst-case situation: she only needed to bide her time for another day, when she and Nick were already set to leave for London. The better solution was to find a reason to leave first thing in the morning.

Amelia looked around her, having a hard time believing her run-in with Shauley had left her mostly unharmed.

Before she made it to the courtyard, another horse approached. She whirled around, expecting to see Shauley with murder in his expression but was surprised to spy Nick galloping toward the inn like his heels were on fire.

She'd never been more relieved to see him—or more angry at the same time.

"Did you seek what you were so adamant in finding?" She couldn't help her wicked tongue.

Nick came down from his horse and reached for her hand to pull her close. "I'm sorry for charging out of here as I did."

"I haven't decided if I can forgive you yet." She cleared her throat. Admittedly, she felt immense guilt for thinking poorly of him and the circumstance that brought them both to this impasse. "Huxley arrived nearly two hours ago, Nick."

She wanted to ask why he'd been gone so long, but she didn't want to pry into his whereabouts too much since she already had an idea of where he'd been.

"So he wasn't held up as long as he thought," Nick said carefully, looking at her and the field of grass around them.

"No," she said shortly, her temper getting the better of her. Their conversation felt oddly stilted, and Amelia realized there was a lot unsaid between them that they would have to sort out before their marriage would ever run smoothly.

She thought back on Shauley's warning that she remain quiet. No easy feat when she had promised to remain honest out of respect to her husband.

"I requested that the kitchen set aside a late dinner for us," she said, unsure of whether she should ask him more about the incident that had separated them in the first place.

Despite knowing the reason, clarity and the truth from him might have the ability to set them both on a better path, one that didn't put them at odds.

Amelia nearly snorted on reflection; they'd remain at odds as long as there were secrets between them, and she was nothing but a hypocrite to think she wouldn't have to divulge her conversation with Shauley in return for her husband's honesty.

"Walk with me to the stables," Nick said. The firmness of his expression told her that it wasn't a request.

Nick glanced over his shoulder before placing the flat of his hand on her lower back and guiding her deeper into the courtyard. *Toward safety*, she couldn't help but think. Her deep inhalation was shaky, and she hoped her husband didn't notice the nervousness that infused her.

She couldn't take the awkwardness stretching between them any longer. "Where have you been, Nick? You left nearly two hours ago, and you're only going to ask me to walk to the stables with you?"

"I should ask you the same thing. I saw you walking back. Did I not advise you of the danger in going anywhere alone?"

Two wrongs do not make a right, she wanted to say, but bit her tongue.

"I was enjoying an evening stroll, wondering where my husband could have gone. Thinking I would find you but it appears fortune was not on my side until I turned back. Do not turn this around. I asked a legitimate question, and I expect an honest answer."

"Amelia." There was censure in his tone.

"Perhaps you shouldn't have left as you did. Don't you dare lecture me when it was you who stormed out of here like a demon possessed by some unknown urge toward vengeance."

Nick took up her hand and kissed the back of it. "I'm sorry," he said. There was a hint of sincerity in his voice, but that didn't excuse his behavior.

Or hers.

She hated herself for the lie, even if it was only an omission of the truth. But she would never get the answers she needed if she let this go.

"Don't you think if that were the truth, you would explain why the monk's appearance in my day had you running out of here with some madman's purpose?"

The stable boy approached head down and looking uncomfortable as he took the reins from Nick's hands. His approach stopped her from saying anything more.

"A conversation better saved for when we are alone," Nick said gently.

"And I asked you not to lecture me." She dislodged her hand from his hold. "You may come and find me when you have something worthwhile to tell me."

With that, she turned away and left him standing just outside the stable. Leaving the way she did was the start of a brilliant plan. A way to lure him away from Highgate by the ridiculous imposed deadline Shauley had given her. She would not fail in this task. She could not. Not at the risk of either of their lives. Not at the risk of losing what they had built over the last month.

She was reminded again that it was no easy feat to succeed at marriage. It took work. Hard work. And she hoped that her white lie would turn out to be a benefit to them both.

CHAPTER SEVEN

Nick never imbibed freely of spirits. On occasion, he could tolerate a good deal of any fiery liquid poured down his throat, and drink any man under the table, but tonight...tonight he couldn't seem to pull back. More to the point, he didn't want to. He wanted to be lost in his cups, to forget why he was here. To forget his purpose in purchasing Caldon Manor.

His shoulder hit the wall on the curve of the stairs, and he fell heavily on the next step.

"Bloody fool, you are." Huxley's stern voice barely made it through the grog and fog in Nick's head.

He slurred a string of words together, and Huxley got the gist of it.

"You aren't sleeping in my room. You'll have to see your wife, let her ring you out and twist your ear for being an idiot. Don't think you've had this much to drink in nigh on fifteen years, and then only after you won a fight that resulted in grave injuries for the other party."

"Needing…needs…" Nick pointed his finger at his friend, trying to bring his grim face into focus. "I don't need reminders, Huxley."

Huxley's shoulder came up under Nick's arm, supporting most of his weight.

"Bloody heavy bloke, you are. Should just leave you here for the missus to find you, come morning."

"I appreciate your help." Nick's side hit the wall again. Amelia was not going to be happy to see him in this state. Getting lost in spirits had seemed like a good idea at the time.

Still didn't seem half bad, though he doubted he would make it back downstairs still standing.

But he'd angered his wife, and even he could admit he'd lost track of his purpose in coming to Highgate. He had tried to confront his past only to fail. So now what was he supposed to do?

"So many questions."

"What are you yammering on about?" Huxley said.

"Amelia asks so many questions."

"Drunk as a bloody lout. I hope you do regret this, come morning."

"I will be fine."

"You come see me at the crack of dawn and tell me that with the same conviction and I will never doubt you again."

Huxley tossed him down on the floor in front of the rooms he shared with Amelia. His friend knocked on the door. They waited for what felt like forever. Perhaps it was forever, or even only a few minutes. He couldn't be sure. Sleep could find him anywhere right now. Mindless sleep. That was what he needed a night of. A mindless, numbing sound sleep, one without interruption. One without dreams.

When Amelia didn't answer the door, Huxley tried the knob, which didn't turn. At least she'd locked it before going to bed. Though now, he was locked out of his own room. There was a certain amount of humor in that, and he couldn't help but chuckle.

Huxley cuffed him up the side of the head, making Nick's ears ring. "People are sleeping so shut it, or I'll toss you into the stables to sleep with the animals."

"Shh," Nick said to his friend and pushed his back against the wall next to the door. "Wait. I have a key." He patted down his waistcoat pocket, his jacket pockets, but couldn't seem to locate what he was looking for.

Huxley searched Nick's pockets with quick efficiency and pulled out the key to Nick's room. "See, there it is." Nick smiled up at his friend, but Huxley did not return the gesture; if anything, his frown deepened the lines on his forehead.

"If we wake Amelia, you get to explain to her what happened," Huxley lectured him.

"I can do that," Nick said as his friend unlocked the door and let it swing open. It was dark inside, almost like the room was beckoning Nick to step inside its warm, embracing arms and sleep comfortably, contently.

His wife, his bed…sleep. When was the last time he'd had a full night's rest? He couldn't recall.

"I don't think you ever slept a night like a babe on a woman's breast," Huxley said in response to Nick's thoughts.

No, that didn't seem right. "Said that out loud?"

"You did. Now shut your trap before you wake your wife. Are you going to get up off the floor, or am I going to have to carry you to your own bed?"

Nick pushed his friend away when he attempted to help Nick to his feet.

"I can do this myself," he said.

Huxley backed off, hands raised to indicate Nick was free to do as he pleased.

Nick pushed himself off the floor, none too elegantly, but he held on to the frame of the door and hauled himself up to a standing position.

He already felt a headache coming on, a testament of just how much he'd imbibed this evening. He covered his eyes with one hand. "Definitely going to regret this in the morning."

"I told you that five whiskeys ago."

Nick stood there, holding the frame of the door to keep his world from spinning, and looked at his friend though half-lidded eyes. Nick let go of the wall so he could point his forefinger at his friend. "You did me a service tonight. I'll sleep like a babe. Be the first time in…in a long time."

"Well, get to bed, then, so I can find my own mattress for the night."

"Thank you."

"You won't be thanking me come morning."

"Maybe not, but still needs to be said. You're a good friend, Huxley. And I doubt I'd have made it this far without you."

"You certainly wouldn't have made it up the stairs."

Nick thought Huxley wore a smirk before turning away, but he couldn't tell with his head spinning the way it was. He pushed himself through the doorway and into the room, stumbling toward the bed as he removed articles of clothing and let them drop to the floor. He wasn't sure all of them came off before he hit the bed like a bag of rocks. What he did know was that Amelia didn't curl into him as she always did, and that absence left a cold spot in his chest that he rubbed at until he fell asleep.

Amelia tilted her head to the side and stared down at her husband lying face down in their bed. He'd managed to pull off his jacket and waistcoat—those lay dejectedly on the floor where he'd tossed them on entering last night—but his shirt and trousers and his boots were still on.

While her temper had long ago cooled, the sight of his obvious drunken bout overnight did not bode well for her husband.

She'd honestly contemplated a bucket of cold water over his head to wake him, but that seemed cruel, and she didn't want to explain to the proprietor of the inn what had happened. Though the owners likely already knew what her husband had been up to last night, because Nick certainly hadn't been drinking in their room while she slept.

It was nearing ten in the morning, and Landon had sent a note an hour ago, asking when Nick wanted to reschedule their meeting. A small voice in the back of her head reminded her that she'd never seen Nick sleep so soundly. It would serve him right if she left him here to sleep the remainder of the day, but that might mean they stayed tomorrow as well.

She hated to do it, but he had left her with no choice. Placing her knee on the bed to give her leverage, and wrapping her hands around his solid arms, she rolled him over and onto the floor. He hit it hard, making her cringe and feel a moment of regret.

She reminded herself that he had brought this on himself.

This was his fault, not hers. And he hadn't responded to any of her verbal requests to wake up.

"What in hell?" he grumbled, still half asleep. His hand grasped the edge of their bed, and Nick pulled up to a sitting position.

Amelia had already scooted away from the bed and taken a moment to compose herself. She placed one hand on her hip as she waited for Nick to make it to his feet.

He threw his arm over his eyes to block the light that was blinding him. She'd opened the curtains an hour ago, hoping the morning light would wake him.

She almost felt sorry enough to close them again.

Almost.

"I would apologize, but it's after ten, and you have missed your morning obligations. Landon sent a note for you an hour ago, and I felt it necessary to make excuses for you. Seeing you now, I wish I hadn't."

Nick rubbed his hand over his eyes and peeked through a crack in his fingers.

"You look a little green this morning, husband. If this is going to be a common occurrence, I'd appreciate your telling me now. Because I certainly didn't realize I was marrying a man who spent the whole night out on a binge."

Nick lowered his hand and gazed at her through narrowed eyes. "I can promise you did not."

Amelia raised one eyebrow. She would not state the obvious. Surely he knew how bad this looked.

"What time did you say it was?"

With a huff, she lowered her hand and walked over to his waistcoat that had been tossed in the middle of the floor. She pulled out his watch, clicking it open.

"Twenty after ten."

"I hadn't expected to be asleep so long."

Amelia held out the note Landon had sent up.

Nick waved it away. "What does it say?"

"That he would be pleased to see you before we take our next meal. Though by the looks of you, I doubt you'll stomach anything at present."

"No, nothing right now." Nick stretched, the material of his shirt molding to his arms. He looked down at himself, as though just realizing he hadn't undressed before falling in bed.

"I admit to being surprised you didn't wake me last night. You probably stumbled all the way to bed."

"You are no more surprised by that than I am." Nick rubbed his bloodshot eyes again. He sat heavily on the edge of the bed and put his head in his hands.

"I'll ring for a bath."

"I haven't the time."

"You'll make time. You smell like the ale house you were in all night."

"That bad?" He turned his head to look at her with bloodshot eyes.

"Yes. And don't think because you are ailing this morning from yesterday's overindulgence that I have forgiven you for walking out yesterday."

"I haven't."

"Haven't what?" Amelia walked around the bed so she wasn't talking to his back.

"Amelia, as much as I know we need to have this conversation, now is not going to work."

"If that's the case, we will get on disagreeably, if for no other reason than your obstinacy."

Amelia shut her eyes and took a deep breath as she counted to five. He was feeling the effects of the evening and would probably be an irritable companion for the remainder of the day.

Nick grasped her hand and pulled her closer. "I apologize for my state this morning. And to answer your earlier question, no, this is not usual for me."

Wanting nothing more than to remain in charge of the situation and refusing to be placated by more promises from him, she said, "That has yet to be proven."

"Fair enough," he responded and released her to stand. He looked in pain, but he'd brought this upon himself and she refused to help him right now.

"Might I ask for what reason you imbibed so freely?" And carelessly, she wanted to say but didn't.

"You know why."

"You have ordered me to stay away from the monk without providing a reason. Should I guess your intentions? I will give you this one last chance to tell me what is going on, or I will head back to London this instant."

It wasn't a fair tactic to use when he was at a great disadvantage, but she had to use whatever leverage was available to her. Shauley's words were fresh in her mind, and she would heed his warning, if for no other reason than the fact that she still lived.

Either the conviction in which she made her threat or the words alone were enough, Nick caught her hands and pulled her suddenly into his large frame. On impact, she let out an oomph sound.

"I don't care if I reek like a man who swam in a barrel of cheap wine more odious than the Thames after it rains. You need to listen to me carefully, Amelia."

She didn't release the hold she had on his arms. She wished all this was behind him, that the sudden worry she felt for his safety was a thing of the past. If only Shauley hadn't escaped after she'd been saved, then none of this would have been as big an issue as it had grown to be.

"I've been listening all along, Nick. And I could do without the manhandling." Even though it was Nick, her husband, and the only man she loved, she was getting sick of being tossed around like rag doll.

He released her just as quickly as he'd gathered her close. She didn't move away, but stood her ground, breathing as heavily as a thoroughbred after a race won. Every inhalation caused her breasts to brush against his chest.

"I'm sorry for my actions, Amelia." Nick's voice softened. "This place has the ability to strip away my humanity one layer at a time. I hate feeling like my back is exposed, waiting for the right enemy to happen by and strike me down. I'm nothing more than a moving target."

"Do you think I hadn't noticed what this place was doing to you? Your nightmares have been more frequent, Nick. You haven't had a full night's sleep since we arrived—not counting last night."

Before he could make further excuses, she raised her hand between them. Nick's words died on his lips. Finally, she had his full attention. Perhaps she was making headway.

"I love you. And I would hope that held some sort of weight. That you could trust me with your secrets."

"Your love is everything to me. Everything," he responded.

"If that were true, you wouldn't be chasing ghosts and letting your past consume you. While you've been watching me, Nick, I've been watching you. Whatever it is you are afraid to tell me, it's eating you up from the inside out, one day at a time. I see what this place is doing to you. It's cutting you down, piece by piece. It's destroying you. I want to help, but I can't if you won't let me in."

"If you want the truth—"

"You know that's all I have ever wanted from you."

"I left a piece of myself here years ago," he said carefully, as though thinking his words out before saying them.

"You didn't, Nick. You might think you did, but you are stronger than that."

"This place stole my innocence, which would have eventually been taken, considering the place and life I lived."

"And isn't that the exact point you are missing?"

Nick scratched at his scalp, further mussing up his deliciously tumbled hair. Why she was attracted to him in his current disheveled state was beyond her.

"I have had to set this right for more years than I care to count," he explained.

"By facing your demons directly, instead of working on letting go of your past."

"Give me today, Amelia. There is one more thing I need to accomplish before we leave."

"But to what end? Honestly, Nick, you are a good man without dredging up the hatred inside left from your past.

And the man I met and got to know…that's the man I adore beyond measure. Not this person you become when chasing a past that no longer has bearing on the person you are now."

Amelia draped a shawl over her arm and walked toward the door. "Do find me when you've cleaned yourself up."

She left, because if she stood there another moment, arguing the merits on seeking out his revenge, it would only further frustrate her. He would have to make his own decision in this. So close…she had been so close to getting him to leave, she'd felt it, noted it in the way he'd tensed up when she'd threatened to leave for London.

When she arrived in the inn's dining area, she saw Meredith and almost turned back around to avoid the conversation they needed to have. She almost groaned her dismay. Her day wasn't looking up in the least.

Meredith motioned to the seat next to her. Pasting a smile on her face, Amelia approached the table.

"I see we are both without our husbands this morning."

"Indeed," Amelia said tightly as she slid out a chair. "Have you already eaten?"

"Yes, I was down early this morning."

"I assume you are also leaving Highgate today?"

"We are not. My husband is touring the properties, speaking with the families and business owners. Determining who to keep, and weeding out any problem tenants."

One of the inn's daughters came by their table. "Another serving of tea, my lady?" she asked of Lady Burley.

"Yes, for my friend here. I might as well have another too."

The maid dipped her head and left them alone.

"I thought we were leaving today or tomorrow, but Nick might have some further business to take care of first."

"About yesterday—"

"Think nothing of it, Lady Burley."

"Please, call me Meredith." The look that crossed Meredith's face was a cross between distress and sadness. "I think it only fair that I explain my actions yesterday."

"There's honestly no need."

Despite Amelia's insistence that they had nothing to discuss, Lady Burley continued. "Do you know how our husbands met?"

Amelia decided she might as well play along. The faster Lady Burley said what she needed, the faster she could get on with her day. "They were rival owners, constantly bidding against each other."

Meredith hesitated. "That's a very small part of how they became friends."

Amelia's teacup was set down on the table with a fresh pot of tea. Amelia thanked the maid before focusing her attention back on Meredith.

"You have my attention." She didn't mean to sound short, but yesterday's picnic had left a bad taste in her mouth. She busied her hands with the tea set, pouring out another cup for Meredith before making her own.

"When they were younger, they were more apt to make calculated moves, more so than they might make today."

"The same can be said for almost any man caving a path of his own in life."

"To an extent, though their past is a slight bit darker than that."

"Yes, it is," Amelia agreed.

"Our husbands met during a fighting match." Meredith paused, nibbling on her lower lip. "Not the kind in which gentlemen engage at a pugilist club."

"I know precisely how Nick started out, how he made his 'reputation,' if you will." She didn't need to get into the finer details of what that life might have been like, for she wasn't there firsthand to experience it. The truth of the matter was that Amelia knew more about her husband than Meredith did, no matter what the other woman thought.

"I did not mean to imply otherwise," Meredith said without an ounce of affront. "I never thought I would marry Landon," she said almost wistfully. "It was happenstance. I was, in fact, waiting on a proposal from another man entirely. Landon and I were worlds apart and at one point stood for different things. He and my eldest brother, Shelley, were as close as any brothers could be."

Amelia did not miss the note of sadness that inflected Meredith's voice. It was also hard to miss the shake of her hand as she took a sip of her tea.

"Were?" Amelia dared to query the tense in which Meredith referred to the friendship she mentioned.

"Shelley died rather suddenly. He just didn't wake up one day." Lady Burley's eyes grew misty, and Amelia felt awful about being cold to her.

"I'm sorry."

"I've had plenty of time to come to terms with the unfairness of the world and of life, Amelia."

Amelia agreed with that sentiment for so many reasons, none of which she would share with her tea companion.

"Landon took it as hard as Shelley's own flesh and blood. He wasn't himself after that. I guess it's hard to be when death stares you so coolly in the face and changes the way things are. He got into a lot of brawls and tavern fights that my other brothers had to break up. Landon moved to London not a fortnight after the funeral."

"I know what it's like to want to escape the place that you feel is responsible for your circumstance," Amelia said, thinking that a little empathy might go a long way.

She hated to have the same sentiments as Meredith after yesterday's disastrous lunch, but Amelia knew she would have acted the same way, had their roles been reversed. How could she fault Meredith for that?

"He met Nick after that, didn't he?" Amelia asked, already figuring out part of the story.

Meredith surprised Amelia with a chuckle. "Fought him, actually. And by my husband's account, Nick knocked him flat on his rear in mere seconds. Landon stayed out of fighting after that, but he continued to watch with the same morbid fascination one might get from a cock fight."

"I can't say I see the pleasure in either."

"I couldn't agree more."

"How did they become rivals in business?" Amelia asked, never having thought to ask Nick that very question in the past, as it was neither here nor there.

And now, her curiosity was truly piqued by what Meredith revealed. Amelia realized in that moment how starved for information on her husband she truly was. She pressed forward, wanting to know every tidbit of information.

"They have similar ideas on where to invest, so when their paths continually crossed, they realized it would be better to work together instead of against each other."

"Help me understand Roberts's position…" Amelia eyed the man who stood in the background, even now. He wasn't like any servant she had ever known or seen.

Meredith grinned. "My husband has probably nearly as many enemies as Nick has. They are savvy with their business dealings, sometimes undercutting peers who feel entitled to something they cannot necessarily afford."

"Like Murray's property."

"Exactly."

"Has your husband found trouble before?"

"He nearly lost his life on one occasion. I'm not willing to repeat such an event for as long as I live. Death will not part my husband and me prematurely. I could not bear it."

Amelia felt the same way with Nick, and when she thought back on his actions of late, the feeling was most certainly reciprocated.

Tipping the last sip of tea into her mouth, she then set the dainty white cup down on her saucer. "Thank you for the conversation, Meredith. It does go a long way toward my seeing you in a more…appreciative light."

"I did not mean to give you the wrong impression yesterday." Meredith's words were sincere, but Amelia had been too trusting of late and decided to err on the side of caution. There was no reason to rush into anything. She smiled at Meredith.

"Nick and I will return to London tomorrow," Amelia said.

"We will not be far behind you. I think we'll be down in a couple of days."

"Then perhaps we can arrange a breakfast…or an evening soiree." Could she be so daring? Yes, yes, she could.

"That would be lovely. And thank you for spending some of your morning with me, when I'm sure this was the last thing you wanted to do."

"It's been a pleasure."

Amelia slid her chair out from the table, checked the tie on her bonnet, and nodded her good-bye to Meredith.

While she probably should have asked someone to come along with her, considering Shauley's appearance last night, she wanted time alone. She wasn't ready to see her husband, and she couldn't face Huxley just yet, knowing that he was the one to bring Nick back to their room. Did Huxley know that she and Nick had fought? No, she definitely could not face him.

If she stayed within the village area, where quite a few people milled about at this hour, she was unlikely to see Shauley. And that suited her perfectly well. It also gave her some time to come up with a plan to get her husband to leave Highgate today. And if she couldn't get him to leave, then she'd have to find reason to keep them both in their room until the morrow. Not too hard a task, she thought, sure she wore a silly grin on her face at the prospect of staying abed with her husband for another day.

Nick would probably be a few hours in washing up, meeting with Landon, and eating—if he could stomach it—which gave her enough time to come up with said plan. And it also kept her from running back to him to tell him everything that had happened to her the night before. She was torn in her lies. Torn in what she should do. But it felt right to withhold her meeting with Shauley for the time being. She would reevaluate that decision later.

Chapter Eight

After a long soak in the hipbath, Nick's megrim had subsided, and his spirits were a little higher with the day ahead. Amelia hadn't come back to their room, which, to him, said she was avoiding him. So be it; he hadn't been pleasant on waking this morning. Although he knew he would have to fix what he'd done wrong later in the day.

Dressing quickly, he made his way down to the stables to procure a horse for the day. Landon could wait, and he didn't want to face Huxley just yet.

While Amelia might not appreciate that he had to do this, there simply was no way for him to avoid what he'd been working toward for the past year. And it had to be done before they left Highgate.

The memories of what this place represented needed to end—the terrors he woke to in the night that still had the ability to haunt him and his thoughts constantly turned to this place whenever he thought about building the school. Screaming at him that this was a momentous mistake. Nick well knew that he would never find closure if his business with the vicar didn't take precedence. If he didn't face the only man who had ever frightened him.

He left the village without looking back. There was no time to think about this without acting; it had to be done. The sooner he did this, the sooner he could explain it to Amelia, and the sooner he could wash his hands of this place and the hold it had over him. At least, that was what he hoped.

The horse he rode frothed and champed at the bit, eager to be let loose, but Nick kept him at a steady pace so that neither of them would be injured once they entered the wood. He easily found the trail that led him to the *monk's* cabin. That Amelia had spent time with one of the men from his childhood…it had him seeing red. Unintentionally, his heels dug into the horse's side, and it reared up, stopping them in their tracks. Nick loosened his legs and gave the beast gentle strokes over its thick neck. "Sorry, Handsome." Nick was sure a child had named the beast of a horse. "Didn't mean to frighten you."

"Two strangers in so many days" came a cracked voice that obviously belonged to an old man.

Nick spun his horse, looking for the source, and halted when he spied the man he'd been looking for last night.

"Brother John." It was amazing that he could forget many faces after years of not seeing them, but not this man's, who had been the old curate at the school. The man's face was etched into his brain, so deep it was just another scar like those that marked his back.

"Do I know you, son?" The man gave him a quizzical glance.

Nick swung his leg over the horse and jumped to the ground. He towered over the man now; how odd to remember having been a frightened, small boy when he'd last seen the curate.

"I attended St. Vincent's as a youth."

On closer inspection, Nick saw the man's eyes were clouded and hindering, though obviously the man was not blind. He wore monk's robes, the material so old that it was tattered, patches sewn into the bottom hem. While ragged and threadbare, it was clean, and by all appearance worn of a humble servant of God. Nick nearly snorted with that thought but refrained.

"St. Vincent's you say? That's more than twenty years past. School closed when the vicarage was replaced by another church."

Nick stood a few feet away from the man, not willing to get too close, afraid of what he might do, as the man obviously didn't know him from Adam. "Yes, twenty years. Though it was a long time ago, I remember it like it was yesterday. Do you live out here alone?"

Brother John waved Nick closer, but Nick couldn't stand to be too close to him and backed up a step. "Walk with an old man for a while, son."

Nick bristled at the familiar name. "I am not your son."

"We are all sons in the eyes of the Lord."

Nick made a noise in the back of his throat but stayed his tongue, biting back something harsh and foul. The men who had been a part of that school were no sons mindful of God's work; they were all disciples of the devil.

The old man didn't wait for Nick; he ambled carefully down the path with his cane, stopping to uncover some mushrooms, picking them, and then continuing on. He didn't seem to care if Nick followed or not.

Nick followed, because this was a means to the end. This was the first step in getting what he came here for.

"You met my wife yesterday," Nick told him.

"Ah, yes. What a kind woman. She graciously assisted me home, even when I refused to take her away from her daily tasks."

Nick would not play games with this man; their idle chit-chat needed to come to an end. "Surely you know who I am."

"I do. You're the man who bought Caldon Manor. It's about time that property was taken on by someone who cares about its future. Your wife said you would be investing in the house."

Nick was forced to trail behind, as Brother John continued on his path without waiting or beckoning Nick to accompany him again. This conversation wasn't the one he expected, and to Nick's surprise, the anger that had built in him throughout the day started to dissipate. How odd it was to not hate the man before him.

"She tells the truth," Nick said, scratching the back of his head, wishing he knew how to approach the topic he'd come here to discuss.

"A grand house like that shouldn't fall to such a state of disrepair. It's good that someone wants to commit the necessary funds. You should have seen it in its heyday."

That made Nick wonder just how long the curate had lived here, because the house hadn't been in prime condition when he was a youth, though it fared a hell of a lot better twenty years ago than it did today.

Nick had nothing to say to that as he walked a few feet behind Brother John. "Do you not remember me?" he asked, finding their conversation odd and unplanned. Nick found himself nearly speechless.

"I'm sorry, son. I do not."

The answer caught Nick off guard. What did you say to a man who didn't remember you, even when you hated him beyond everything?

Nick was not here to enjoy a stroll through the wood at midday. He was here to get answers…to find the vicar.

To exact his revenge.

That was the only reason he was here, and he could not forget that purpose.

Nick wondered what he would say to the vicar, now that so much time had passed. What if the vicar didn't remember him either? It didn't matter; what mattered was confronting the man who had destroyed his childhood and getting answers as to why. Then he would get a confession out of the bastard for all his misdeeds and have him arrested by the magistrate, because there could be no other end for a man as vile as the vicar.

"Are you sure you don't remember me?" Nick asked.

"When you've lived to be as old as I am, you'll find your memory starts to change. I can remember my childhood with perfect clarity; it's the part in between that has grown foggy."

Nick wanted to say it was because the curate wanted to forget his dark past just as much as Nick did, but he would not paint this man in a friendlier light.

"You helped destroy the lives of so many. Surely you remember your role at the school? Your purpose in luring boys, unaware of what they were in for? Of supporting the depravity of your brothers at the vicarage?"

Brother John stumbled in the path, and Nick, hating himself more and more by the second, helped the bugger right his footing until he could steady himself once again with his cane.

"Thank you," Brother John said.

"Is that all you have to say to me?"

"Hallo!" called a third party.

That voice.

Nick spun away from the curate and stormed toward the man he despised as much as he did the vicar.

"Shauley," he growled as though he were cursing something vile.

"Nicholas," Shauley responded, a decided lack of venom that didn't go unnoticed, considering they had parted with harsh words the last time they'd seen each other. Considering this man would soon suffer the same pain Amelia had. He owed Shauley that much and more.

"I'm within my rights to take you to the magistrate," Nick said—but why had he said that? He approached within ten feet or so of his quarry. He wished he had something to fight with, something to knock Shauley off his horse and put him on even ground.

"You can try." Cocky as ever, Shauley had that same attitude as a boy, as though he was invincible. Well, he had another think coming.

"There's a bounty for your capture, Shauley."

"Your own contribution filled that fund, I'm sure."

Not precisely, though Nick offered to double anything the magistrate was willing to put up.

Nick turned his focus back to the monk, but the man had exited at some point after Shauley's arrival. Damn it. He'd been so close to finding the vicar. He'd have to find Brother John again, now that he'd been interrupted. And that meant Amelia would be angry with him, more so than she was now, when he told her they needed to stay another day.

As Nick edged toward his horse, needing to either ride out of here like hellhounds were nipping as his feet or give chase to the monster standing in front of him.

"You're helping them, aren't you?" Nick asked, suddenly realizing Shauley's presence was no coincidence.

"By 'them,' I assume you mean Brother John and Reverend Andrew."

The closer Nick got to his horse, the farther Shauley seemed to back up his mount. Nick wasn't sure what he'd do to his old foe, should he catch him, and he didn't flinch at the idea of killing Shauley with his bare hands; in fact, he wasn't so sure he could pull himself back if given that opportunity. Nick could envision it perfectly—his hands around Shauley's throat, choking the last breath out of his beaten body.

"Was that your mark or the inspector's heavy handprint left on my wife's face?" Nick cracked his knuckles, ready to fight this out if that's what it came to. Hell, he wanted to fight this out, retribution for the pain Shauley had caused his wife.

"How does Mrs. Riley fare?"

Nick rolled his shoulders. There was no way in hell Shauley was getting out of here in one piece. But first, he'd have to catch the slimy eel. The reins of Nick's horse were within reach. Nick could either casually climb onto the horse, or...

"I wouldn't bother," Shauley said, pulling a pistol from his saddlebag and pointing it at Nick's chest.

"I asked you a question, Shauley." Nick was at his wit's end. Did he take a chance or hold his ground? He eyed the pistol. Shauley's aim was steady and direct.

"And I chose not to answer," Shauley snapped back, his temper now getting the better of him. Nick hoped that would be to his advantage, because when Shauley was angry, he could make a misstep that would give Nick a momentary advantage.

"Why are you here?" Nick had to try another angle because he certainly had no intentions of standing here all day, helpless to act on every front.

"You're interfering with my plans."

"The same could be said of you."

"I suppose you're right." Shauley came closer, the pistol never wavering.

"Did they teach you to shoot in school as well as give you a fondness for young boys?"

"I feel sorry for you, Nick. If you look at yourself, your life, your history, what do you see of the man you are? You're weak, even though you will not admit it. You're pathetic, in that you try to hide from your past. What is the reason you purchased this shit hellhole of land? There's nothing left here for either of us. You moved on a lot sooner than I ever did. I stayed here. I endured. This is my battle to fight, not yours, when you gave up the opportunity time and time again."

"Is that what this is about? Because you couldn't escape the school and what the teachers thought we needed to be educated in? It's my fault you ended up the way you did?" Nick nearly snorted in laughter.

Shauley shook his head. "We are more similar than you think."

"Not in the least."

Shauley ignored him. "I don't blame you for getting out of here at the first opportunity. Had my mother a care in the world, I wonder if she would have withdrawn me, even after I insisted on staying. But she didn't. And here we are. Together, in the middle of the bloody Highgate forest where the downfall of our childhood took place."

And that was the crux of the matter that had destroyed their friendship. They'd never talked about what had happened to them as boys, but the knowledge always stood between them. The hatred for what had happened to them and the anger and frustration that they had no control to stop it.

"Did they make you believe it was normal?" Nick asked, truly curious as to why Shauley would stay behind when Nick's own mother had advocated bringing him home to St. Giles at Nick's insistence. None of it had mattered. Shauley had already made up his mind. He'd stayed. Nick had run away. He hated to think that made him the weaker person, but it was hard to see it in any other light.

"Normal? Sodomizing young boys? Definitely not. When I think back on it all, my reasons for staying made me no better than my mother. I whored myself out, thinking it would get me to a better place in life, give me the opportunities I would not otherwise have as the son of a harlot. I stuck through it all because it was a free education; it was the name of a vicarage behind me when I entered the workforce." Shauley closed his eyes and inhaled deeply before gazing directly at Nick again. "And then there's you…"

Nick would not justify the position he'd gained in his life. He and Shauley were worlds apart. "I'm sure we have both done regrettable things in our lives," Nick said.

"It's not envy I feel. It never has been. You've been little more than a nuisance in my life. Until the Murray deal, that is."

Nick didn't think it was as simple as that either. Regardless of all else, Nick had been the one to escape. Nick alone had been free of the abuse suffered at the hands of the men of the vicarage where they'd gone to school.

"If you didn't harbor any ill will toward me, then why did you take Amelia?"

"As I said, you're getting in the way of my plans. I needed your attention elsewhere, though it didn't seem to work, aside from forcing your hand in marriage."

Nick would not enlighten Shauley to the fact that Nick had wanted to marry Amelia, regardless of the fact that they'd been caught sleeping in the same bed. When the opportunity to marry her had presented itself, he hadn't shied away from it. She was now irrevocably his.

Nick crossed his arms over his chest. This conversation was going 'round and 'round without actually accomplishing anything. What he needed was to disarm Shauley. But how? The bloody pistol was still pointed in the center of Nick's chest, directly over his heart. He was a dead man if he didn't play his cards carefully.

"If you want me to stay out of your way, you'll have to tell me what I'm getting in the way of."

Shauley slowly shook his head. "What kind of fool do you take me for? If I tell you my plan, you'll find a way to ruin it. Not a chance I'm willing to take."

"You have to throw an old dog a bone, Shauley. I will not be stopped from accomplishing what I came here to finish."

"You'll have to finish it another day."

"Why are you helping them?"

Shauley's smile was menacing and ugly. "Is that what you think I'm doing?"

"Being cryptic doesn't tell me anything other than the fact that you're still an ass who thinks himself superior to all his peers."

"Only you can claim that title, my friend. Why else would you spend so much time bloodying people's faces for a few quid?"

It was a sight bit more than a few quid and had started Nick's fortune, but this man deserved no insight into the actions Nick had taken to get ahead in life.

"If you are just going to sit there and threaten me"—Nick motioned toward the pistol—"I'll mount my horse."

"Tsk, tsk. For once, you are not in control of the situation. You don't much like that feeling, do you? Don't make me demonstrate just how much of a disadvantage you have." Shauley's tone was almost apologetic. What did he have to be sorry about?

Nick refused to stand there all day, arguing the merits on who was in a better position to exact revenge on the vicar. He put his foot in the stirrup of his horse at the same moment the pistol cracked, momentarily deafening him.

Nick flew back from the animal as it reared up in reaction to the noise. He was laid out on the ground, whether from the horse or the bullet, he couldn't say, but his shoulder burned, and his arm felt like it was on fire.

"I warned you against taking action." Shauley's voice barely broke through the ringing in Nick's ears. He pressed his hand against the wound on his shoulder.

"Fuck," he groaned, rolling into a sitting position with his good arm pressed against a tree stump. Nick tried to staunch the easy flow of blood coming, but it seemed fruitless since it ran down his arm, wetting his fingers and drip, drip, dripping to the forest floor like the constant beat of a drum.

Being shot was a new experience for him. He'd been in more fights than he could count and even had been put on his ass a few times over the years during those fights with broken bones, a smashed face, and an array of other injuries at one point or another; that was the price one paid for being a fighter. However, none of those incidences compared to the pain radiating through him and rendering him numb right now.

"Always playing the hero. I'd apologize, but I did warn you." Shauley was within spitting distance, and as tempting as it was, some rational bone in Nick's body advised him against it. Right now, Shauley was the only person who knew where Nick was. The bastard held Nick's life in his hands. And Nick had been stupid enough to hand it over without thought.

"I didn't expect you to shoot me."

"And I don't make empty threats." Shauley kicked Nick's foot and came closer, kneeling in front of him. "You always were a stubborn oaf. Serves you right, really."

Was he going to finish him off? All Nick could think was that he wasn't going to see Amelia again. He'd left her in a world where Shauley still existed. A world where she did not have his protection. He blinked, trying to clear his vision.

"So now what?" Nick's words were slurred. He welcomed the familiar tingle of detachment that dulled the ache as his pain sensors kicked in; this was the state of euphoria that used to allow him to continue a fight after being hurt. Though this time, it didn't feel like enough to save him. Too little, too late.

Shauley pulled out a knife from his boot and slid it easily through Nick's jacket, tearing down into the fabric with a hard yank. Nick cringed with renewed pain, but that didn't stop Shauley from his task.

Nick hissed in a breath as Shauley lifted his arm and threaded the fabric under his armpit, tying it at Nick's collarbone. The tightening of the fabric had Nick seeing black, so he took a few steadying breaths and focused his attention on getting the hell out of there.

"Why are you helping me?"

"Who would I have to hate if you were dead? That was just a warning shot." Shauley smacked Nick on his bad arm. "You will live."

Nick hissed in a pained breath.

"Surely you could find someone else to despise."

Shauley chuckled, the sound lighthearted instead of menacing. "But not with a great history like ours. No, my friend, what you don't realize is that we have the same goal."

"Then why aren't we working together?" Though in reality Nick didn't believe that, and he would not work with a man like Shauley willingly.

"Could you imagine anything more absurd?" Shauley was shaking his head, smiling like they were old friends having a conversation over a bottle of bourbon. "We have very different ways of going about things. My way has a lasting effect.

Yours…well, I can't imagine you'd make the vicar suffer as long as I have."

Shauley hauled Nick up to his feet, and Nick swayed, not sure he could walk at all. His vision wavered, his legs nearly gave out, and the drip of his blood hit the ground louder now that he was farther away from it. Odd that he could hear it at all. Maybe it was his heart he heard, keeping up with the speed of his blood loss.

Nick's bad shoulder slapped against the hindquarters of a horse. "I'm not getting you up there alone; you'll have to reach for the pommel."

He was really letting Nick go? It didn't make sense. None of this made sense. It was almost as though he were dreaming this whole scenario between him and Shauley.

Unsure how he did it, Nick pulled himself up onto the horse. The whole ordeal took too much time, and all the while Nick's blood didn't stop, even with the rough tourniquet Shauley had tied around his arm.

With the reins, Shauley tied Nick's hands around the pommel. "Can't have you falling after the effort it took to get you up there," Shauley said by way of explanation.

"Why aren't you finishing me off?" Nick didn't bother to say he wouldn't have been so kind as to let Shauley get away a second time.

"Don't make me regret my decision."

Shauley whacked the rump of the horse, and the animal took off through the forest without Nick's assistance.

The ride was a blur. Nick blinked, trying to keep his eyes open; he didn't steer the horse in any one direction, though it was likely the animal was trained to go back to the inn. For all

Nick knew, Shauley would have a change of heart, catch up to his mount, and shoot Nick dead.

Nick's thoughts went around in his head, constant but slowing. He had to stay awake. He knew if he gave in to his need to sleep, he was a dead man.

He shifted in the saddle, his body sliding to the side but his tied hands keeping him in his seat. He slumped to the side again, straining his injured arm. The burn of pain jarred him fully awake, as it was ten times more painful and throbbing, fierce enough that he threw up. He'd never felt the likes of the megrim that stole his ability to see anything, even in the light of day.

The horse eventually slowed, and Nick had a vague sense of falling. Then there was nothing but blackness as Nick lost his fight with staying awake.

CHAPTER NINE

Amelia handed over a bank note to the milliner. She'd found herself in this lovely shop, wanting to thank the woman for the veil she'd worn on her wedding. Before she knew it, she also had a pair of new gloves, as hers were worn right through.

"The veil was unlike anything I've ever seen. It was the most pleasant surprise, and I cannot thank you enough for having it ready for the wedding."

"That husband of yours paid me well to ensure it was the only concern this shop had. Also told me that it was important to you. Who am I to argue with a man in love?" the proprietress said with a teasing tone. "But my daughter should get more credit, no? She has a fine eye with lace and wanted it to be the best of her work."

The shop owner spoke with a slight accent—either she worked at covering it, or she'd been in England for a long time. She'd guess the woman to be French by the way she rolled her r's when she addressed Amelia. The woman was older, maybe in her forties, with blonde hair that grayed at the temples and swept back into her chignon. Her eyes were as sharp as a young woman's and a beautiful blue that reminded Amelia of sapphires.

"The veil is beautiful. And I'll cherish it until I can pass it down to my children." Should she have children. Now that she thought about it, when was the last time she'd taken her tea to stop from getting pregnant? A few days past, at least. She and Nick hadn't discussed the prospect of children. That was a conversation they would have to have soon. To be on the safe side, she would go back to the inn and have a special brew made. There were a few hurdles they had to navigate before they would be ready to start a family.

The woman behind the counter handed Amelia a card scented with lavender. The shop name was hand lettered in a beautiful scroll that read "Miss Lily's Shoppe for all your fashion needs."

"I do hope you will come by to see me again, Mrs. Riley. I have good connections in France to get the finest of fabrics and designs for the latest fashions."

"I won't be in Highgate much longer, but it would please me to come back soon. I promise you'll be the first person I visit on my return." Amelia didn't tell the milliner that she hated the idea of wasting money on more clothes. However, should the woman want to remain busy and for her business to thrive…Amelia would discuss the option of school uniforms with Nick's sister, Sera.

"Your husband will be building up this town, making it nicer, a more…how do you say? *Sought-after* place to live. I have a feeling you will bring business with you."

"I suppose you're right." Amelia smiled warmly. "I never thought of the impact on the town that restoring Caldon

Manor would bring. There will likely be a lot of workers living this way for a few years. They won't be able to travel from London every day. Though I imagine my husband will hire on people from the village first. I doubt there are enough here for all the tasks required in such a job."

After the house was built, the families of the children who would attend the school would also move into and around Highgate. But Amelia wasn't ready to reveal that part of the plan to anyone just yet. It was only a matter of time, but timing was sometimes everything, and she didn't want any dissenting voices around the school.

A lot of the businesses in this village were rundown, not just from a lack of care but also from a lack of local economy to help them flourish. The population here was stagnant and needed a fresh infusion of blood, new hopes and dreams, something to build this place into a thriving community. While Amelia had no say on which businesses would continue to operate and which would be shut out, she would put in a good word for the milliner. Besides, all towns, small and large, needed one.

"You have a wonderful establishment here, and I'll let my traveling companions know of the excellent service you provide." Perhaps Meredith would stop in and make a purchase to support the shop.

"You're very kind, Mrs. Riley."

Amelia turned to leave, a box with her pair of new gloves in hand. Shopping had lightened her mood a great deal. It was something all for herself and a short reprieve from the troubles that turned over in her mind the past few days. She felt a renewed positivity infuse her. Her anger had dissipated, and she was ready to tell Nick everything. The truth, because she realized that was not something she could keep from him.

The bell over the door rang, and the proprietor's wife from the inn where Amelia roomed ran through the entrance, harried, wringing her hands together in a nervous fashion before wiping the sweat from her brow.

"Miss Lily," the innkeeper's wife said, "you have to come to the inn. There's no time to fetch the sawbones. Bring your bag. It's a gunshot wound."

"Adele," Miss Lily called to the back room, her accent thickening, "Gather the linens from the back cabinet. We will need them with my other pack."

A chill ran through Amelia's whole body and before she could ask what had happened, she was running through the door behind the other women, skirts gathered up in her hands, gloves tucked under her arm. She nearly tripped twice but pulled her skirts higher and continued on, knowing she needed to be there to help. Thank God the inn was close enough that they were there in less than ten minutes.

Amelia barged through the public parlor after the others, breathing hard and needing a second to catch her breath. There was movement everywhere, shouting for order; it was complete chaos. Amelia had to push her way through the crowd that had amassed in the small space. The sight that greeted Amelia was not one she wanted to see, not in a million years.

Nick.

Prone, complexion wan, bleeding; he was spread out on the chaise, his chest rising and falling, his breathing shallow and ragged. Feeling faint, Amelia had to catch herself against the wall. Someone asked if she was all right as they helped her find her footing again.

Miss Lily muttered directions to those standing about, bringing the room to better order. "He needs to be brought up to a room. You and you"—she pointed at two burly men—"take him by the arms and by the feet. He's an ox of a man and won't be easy to move, so I'll tell you once—be careful not to jar him anymore than necessary."

They did as they were told, every step up the stairs bringing to stark light the reality of the situation for Amelia. She followed, wishing she could help more. Feeling useless and unneeded.

How had this happened?

Only this morning they'd been in a heated argument. Part of the new reality of their marriage, with so many lies still hanging between them. None of that mattered now.

None of it.

What mattered was that the last words she'd had with her husband had been venomous. Amelia wiped away the tears that dampened her cheeks. This was her fault.

Amelia ambled after them, keeping her distance as they maneuvered her husband around the staircase and toward their rooms. She pulled the key from her reticule and rushed ahead of them. There were so many people who had helped and followed them into their private chambers that she felt closed in and her breathing came in pants, as though her lungs were starved for air.

She didn't want any of these people in here.

She wanted her husband well. And to be in his arms again. Tears blurred her eyes and washed a path down her face.

"Mrs. Riley, you should wait outside," the proprietor of the inn said, his hand comforting and warm where it gripped Amelia's arm. It did nothing to soothe her fears.

Amelia had the impression he had said it more than once, because he gave her arm a slight shake, the motion forcing her to focus on his wrinkled face. It was enough to clear her jumbled thoughts and snap her out of the fog she'd let herself fall into.

"No. I have to help." She swung into action, making her way through the crowd of people that had gathered.

"You're a healer," Amelia said to the milliner.

"*Oui*," was her response as she used scissors to cut Nick's jacket and shirt away from the wound in his shoulder.

Amelia inhaled sharply on seeing the paleness of his arm and felt her lip tremble when she got her first glimpse of the puckered hole in his arm. It was an ugly wound, bulging and bloody, fleshy and still bleeding. She place her hand against her mouth, sure she was about to lose the breakfast she'd eaten hours ago.

"If you're going to help, I can't have you squeamish," Miss Lily said.

Amelia's eyes snapped over to the lady assisting her husband. She clenched her jaw and took one steadying breath before she got her queasiness under control. "Tell me what to do."

"Cut the rest of his shirt away. I don't want to jar him." She pointed to the hole in his arm. "The blood has slowed since we moved him."

"Is that a good sign?" Amelia had no experience with wounds or illness.

"It depends. I can make you no promises, Mrs. Riley, but I appreciate your assistance." The milliner pressed her ear to Nick's chest. "Heart is beating strong, which means the blood slowed not because his body was weakening. You understand what I'm saying?"

Her face was suddenly in Amelia's.

Amelia nodded and bit the inside of her cheek to keep from crying. Crying would solve nothing. Her husband was strong, his heart healthy, and his body fighting to stay alive.

Miss Lily pointed to the tourniquet tied around his arm and handed a pair of scissors to Amelia. "Might have been worse, had he not done that. Be careful when you cut it; we want to avoid any more bleeding until we remove the bullet."

Amelia finished cutting the last of his shirt away, baring Nick's chest to everyone in the room. There were too many people in here. And she needed to do something about that before she yelled at them all to leave.

"Please, give us some space," she said, shooing everyone out the door.

Landon came running down the hallway just as Amelia got everyone out. She could tell that news had already traveled to him. Landon's expression was set in a furrow of worry, and she could see the questions flitting across his expression, but he said nothing as he watched her approach. She took him by the hand and yanked him into the room, slamming the door shut behind them and cutting off their spectators' curious gazes. This was not a circus act.

"How bad is it?" Landon asked.

"I don't know." She led him over to the bed. "The healer doesn't seem worried."

"I am not. He's done most of the work himself, tying this. Though I think he had help." Miss Lily pointed to the knot at the top before cutting it. "He wouldn't have been able to tie it so tight by himself."

Amelia took Nick's hand in hers. She squeezed it, hoping he would return the gesture, but it lay rough and limp in her hold. She traced the callused tips of his fingers. He was cool to the touch, which didn't seem right.

"Help me turn him over. I need to see where the bullet has gone," Miss Lily instructed.

With the assistance of Landon, the milliner rolled Nick to his side. Adele, who remained silent and at the ready, dipped one of her linens in a bowl of water that was on the washstand and came forward to wipe the back of Nick's shoulder."

"He's clean back here, Mum." There was a thread of worry in the girl's voice, which in turn had Amelia internally fretting. She worried her hands together, hating that she had so little control over the outcome of Nick's fate.

She rubbed Nick's hand between her own hands, wanting to feel the heat back in them. Wanting him to be the one to warm her as he always did. That absence of heat had her lip trembling.

"*Merde*," the milliner said.

While Amelia's French was rusty, she knew the curse for what it was…an incredibly bad sign.

Nick lay on the bed, lifeless. Tears trickled down Amelia's cheek, though she realized she might have been crying this entire time. Tears that came in silence.

"I cannot lose him. Not like this," Amelia said. Landon put his arm around her shoulders. She shook him off; she didn't want to be held by anyone but her husband. She deserved no comfort.

"He's a fighter, this one, Mrs. Riley," Miss Lily said.

"How do you know?" Amelia needed more reassurance that her husband would be fine.

"I will do everything I can to aid him. Everything within my ability." The milliner focused her attention on Landon. "Sir, I will need you to hold him down."

Nick was rolled flat onto the bed, a towel wedged under his bad shoulder. Miss Lily pressed her finger around the wound, eliciting a little more blood. "I cannot feel the bullet on the outside; it's wedged deep," she said.

The healer next stuck her finger in the hole, pushing deep. The sound was sickening, almost unreal. A wave of dizziness washed through Amelia. She grasped the edge of the headboard and squeezed it so hard that the pain shooting through her hand was the only thing keeping her standing. At least that gave her something to focus on.

"You'll have to cut it out," Landon said, still calm and collected. How could he appear so unaffected? Landon rested his hand on Amelia's shoulder, silently asking if she could handle this. She nodded, even though she wasn't so sure. But she refused to leave her husband's side.

"Adele, give me the knife." She held out her hand toward her daughter, waiting for the instrument. "I am not sure if he'll come awake or not, so put all your weight on him."

Landon moved Amelia gently to the side so he was closer to Nick. Kneeling on the bed, he leaned over his friend and applied light pressure to his good shoulder. "Just tell me when."

Without further delay or comment, Miss Lily cut into the wound, making it larger, giving her room to pull out the bullet lodged there. Blood squirted around it; the sound gurgled grotesquely.

Through it all, Amelia held her ground, slowly digesting the fact that her husband needed more from her than the scared girl she had morphed into at the sight of a little blood—well, it wasn't precisely a small amount of blood, but she could be stronger.

Nick needed her. Now more than ever.

And if there was anything Amelia hated more than being helpless, it was being useless. Nick didn't move through the whole ordeal; he lay on the bed, as motionless as her brother had been on the slab of cement at the morgue. She banished the thought as quickly as it came. That would not be Nick's fate, not as long as she lived.

She leaned closer to him and took his hand. While there was little she could do to help in pulling out the bullet, she could provide a presence for her husband. Landon nodded his head, and the small act gave her strength.

"*Les forceps*, Adele," Miss Lily said, extending her open palm toward her daughter.

The healer stuck the long metal instrument into the hole in Nick's shoulder, opening up the tongs as she worked her way deeper. Amelia breathed slowly through her mouth and watched with morbid fascination as the healer rooted around for the object she needed to retrieve.

"*Voilà*," Miss Lily said, her hand working in small movements as she tried to grasp the object. "Get the linens ready, Adele. He's going to bleed like a stuck pig when I pull out the bullet."

The healer's daughter stood at the ready, a stack of linens in her hand. Amelia squeezed Nick's hands harder, knowing that if he should wake during the procedure—as happenstance knew no other time than the moment you least wanted something to occur—she would have to help hold him down. Amelia looked toward Landon; his expression was stern, his hold firm. She hoped it was enough.

They all seemed to wait with bated breath as Miss Lily closed her eyes and focused on what she was feeling through the forceps.

"You see, you need a good grasp before you pull it out. We wouldn't want to leave anything behind." The healer stopped, her focus intense, one hand raised, with her forefinger pointing toward her daughter. "Adele, the spirits."

The girl retrieved a small amber-colored bottle from the bag she'd brought with her. Miss Lily unstopped the cork from the glass container with her teeth and spit it onto the floor.

Everything that happened next transpired so fast, Amelia couldn't say what actually occurred.

The healer's hand tugged hard away from Nick; a small piece of metal glistened red and oozy between the metal forceps. Adele held out a small bowl; the bullet landed in it like a penny dropped in a tin.

The familiar scent of whiskey wafted up from the liquid as it was poured over the wound.

"Now, Adele," the milliner said.

The young girl rushed forward with the linens and pressed them to the enlarged hole in his arm, leaning all her weight into it. The edges of the material quickly soaked up the blood that pumped out of the wound, but it seemed as though the fabric staunched the flow.

Amelia breathed a sigh of relief, even though Nick's journey out of the dark wood had just started. The girl looked to Amelia, a kind expression in her eyes.

"I can hold it, if you have something else you need to do." Amelia placed her hand over the material.

"You cannot just hold it," Adele said. "You must press hard into it, with all your weight."

"As if my very life depended upon it, I will not let up for even a moment," Amelia said and moved around to her husband's side, next to Adele.

Landon loosened his grip, Nick didn't need to be held down anymore; he didn't seem to be waking.

"I'm surprised he didn't rouse," Amelia said.

"He lost too much blood," said Miss Lily. "If he doesn't come down with a fever tonight, he will wake when his body replenishes all the blood he has lost."

"Thank you," Amelia said. "There is no amount of money or gratitude I can give you that will ever be enough for what you have done."

"Don't thank me yet. Your husband has a long road ahead of him."

Amelia climbed up onto the bed, her hand never wavering where it held down the linens.

"You have lived through worse," she whispered to her husband, though she was sure everyone heard her. She didn't care. It needed to be said. So much needed to be said. "We are not yet finished with our argument, and I will not let you off so easily."

The door opened and closed, the proprietor's wife leaving. Amelia recalled the woman refreshing the water in the washstand. She'd said nothing, just acted, provided her services, and left without so much as a word to everyone around her. She was amazing. They all were incredible. Amelia would visit the innkeeper's wife shortly and give her private thanks. Right now, she couldn't bring herself to leave Nick's side.

And to think they had parted with harsh words.

Never again, she vowed.

Never again.

Miss Lily poured water into the dish that held the bullet. She swished it around, turning the water red. She picked up the bullet between a smaller set of forceps and held it up close to the flame of a candle.

"Is it whole?" Landon asked.

"It appears to be."

Amelia didn't miss Landon's sigh of relief. The room collectively seemed more relieved.

Landon took Amelia's hand in his own. "I'll call on my wife to check in on you. I'll need to send letters out about this."

Amelia nodded, a little numb by the events of the afternoon. It was coming up to dark, so they'd been here for some time, even though it had felt like a short while.

"When will I see you next?" she asked Landon.

"Soon. I won't leave you alone through this. Let me send out word. Huxley will likely be up shortly."

Amelia was surprised Huxley wasn't already here. What had kept him away? He was always nearby when Nick seemed to need him most.

Landon was gone before she could voice that concern, and she was left with the healer and her daughter.

"Why are you a milliner if you can heal?"

Miss Lily smiled a little as she approached with a long strip of material and fresh wads of linen. "I trained as a midwife."

"Yet you became a seamstress."

"There was little work for midwives where I was from. I needed to support my family, and that wasn't the way to do it." Miss Lily looked toward her daughter, who was putting away the tools of her mother's trade and pulling out parchments with leaves tucked into the sheaves.

"I am forever indebted to you," Amelia said.

"As I said earlier, don't thank me yet. You have a long night ahead of you." Lily came up on the bed with Amelia, leaning close to the wound on Nick's shoulder, where Amelia still held the linens. Though the cloth felt damp and sodden, she was scared to remove it, afraid the bleeding would start again.

"Come, Adele," Lily said to her daughter. "We'll place the leaves against the wound to help stop the flow of blood.

Adele brought over a small silk satchel of an herb that had long been dried up and crushed inside the bag.

"What is it?" Amelia asked.

"Yarrow. It stops the flow of blood and, once it starts doing its job, we will have enough time to clean around the wound and bandage it."

"Tell me what I need to do."

Lily instructed Amelia on what she needed to do. She helped to clean up Nick and get him bandaged with fresh linens with their assistance. Together, they managed to tie his arm in such a way that when he woke, he wouldn't jostle it and damage it further.

When they were done, Amelia reluctantly left her husband's side. She threw her arms around Lily's shoulders and hugged her tight. "There are no words to express how I truly feel right now."

"You love your husband a great deal. I loved mine that much," the healer said, her hands rubbing up and down Amelia's back in a soothing motion that Amelia appreciated beyond measure.

"I will call on you," Amelia promised. Because of all the women she'd ever met, none were as pure and real as the two women before her.

"You needn't. I will be back as soon as the doctor arrives. He will want to know what we've done for your husband."

Amelia agreed with a nod of her head.

When the door shut behind them, Amelia was at a loss for what to do, how to occupy herself. She turned over the lock, not wanting to be bothered, as she hadn't seen Huxley yet, which seemed odd.

So now what?

Did she wait at the bedside, hoping that Nick woke soon so he could tell her who had done this to him? Though she was sure she knew who was responsible. She knew only one person who would have reason enough to cause her husband harm. Huxley would know how to handle this. Huxley would fix this.

She focused on her husband's lifeless form.

What if Nick didn't wake? She pressed her back to the closed door and just breathed. This first moment of stillness in hours might just be her undoing. Tears trickled out of the corners of her eyes. She didn't sob, though. She didn't scream, even though she felt rage at not being able to turn back the clocks and change the outcome of the afternoon. What if she'd told Nick about her run-in with Shauley? None of this would have happened, had she told the truth. Had she been honest.

She was numb.

Quietly walking over to the bed, she climbed atop the mattress and lay next to her husband, her hand resting over his chest but no other part of her touching him, for she was afraid of hurting him.

CHAPTER TEN

Nick hadn't woken once throughout the night or during the morning as Amelia sat at the bedside, holding his hand, only letting go when someone knocked on their bedchamber door to check on them, to see if there was any improvement with Nick.

She was beside herself with worry.

Sleep never came for her, but she watched Nick, hoping for signs of life, movement, twitches—anything to let her know he would pull through this.

When the healer had stopped in midmorning, she was in the company of a man Amelia did not recognize. He was introduced as a doctor from the neighboring township. And advised Amelia that Nick's doctor in London, who was awaiting his patient's return, had sent him.

"Why didn't Nick's doctor come himself?" Amelia asked.

"He advised that he needed to ready the house for Mr. Riley's arrival. I will ride with you to London, take care of any medical needs that might arise, though I don't believe we have much to worry about."

"Is it safe to move him?"

"Quite. And the doctor there will have greater access to medicine, should a need arise."

Amelia nodded and packed only a bag of necessities for their trip home. Nothing else mattered.

Neither the doctor nor the healer seemed surprised by Nick's state, which helped put Amelia at ease, though only slightly. What she wanted was for her husband to wake and tell her what he needed.

Amelia held herself together by a thread. The only task she had, rolling over and over again in her head, was that Nick needed her.

"Are you sure we shouldn't stay here a while longer?" Amelia asked the doctor. She was actually afraid to move him and cause him more harm.

"Mr. Riley's physician in London is aware of his injuries and will be better equipped to provide for your husband's needs."

The doctor left Amelia with the healer, as he prepared a few items he would need for their trip.

The healer placed her hand atop Amelia's, a gesture of comfort that Amelia needed but didn't feel she deserved. All this was her fault. One white lie, and here her husband lay.

Lily pressed the back of her hand against Nick's forehead. "He is feverish, a sure sign that infection is setting in. I'll help you change the bandages, show you how to clean the wound, but you need to get him back to London before it's too late." The healer stressed the last words with a stern tone that only a mother practiced at scolding a child could achieve. It made Amelia want to do exactly as the healer told her, even though her mind warred with her actions.

Amelia left a note for Huxley, explaining why she'd left, and begged him to send her word, because she was starting to worry that he'd found trouble with Shauley too. She left another note for Lord Burley, letting him know of her concern for Huxley and that she was headed back to London, and then she was off. Hopefully, the post she'd sent on fast delivery would reach the Riley household before she did. All hands would have to be ready to assist with getting Nick up to his room, for that was one thing she could not do alone or even with the help of the doctor.

The carriage ride was horrendous. While the day's weather had started out decently, with the sun rising bright and chasing away the night's frost, rain had rolled in midday to wreak all sorts of havoc on the countryside.

The second time the carriage rolled back in mud and threatened to halt their trip, Amelia got out to assist in pushing the monstrous thing with the driver and doctor. It took them a dozen tries, but with the well-timed aid of the horses hitched to the front, they managed to get it moving forward.

Once they were on the road again, she squished herself in the corner of the leather seat between Nick and the window. Her dress was soaked and her mood dark. She spent the rest of the time supporting Nick's body and keeping him from falling whenever they hit a rut in the rood. The doctor, seated across from her, read a medical journal, but he peered up through spectacles every now and again to assess her husband's state.

Nick's fever hadn't abated, so she pressed her cold hands against him, hoping that his heat would transfer to her and her cold to him. Their situation at present wasn't ideal but was necessary. She wanted to curse the healer for suggesting they leave for London but bit her tongue. None of this was anyone's fault. And she had to trust the doctor across from her.

She rested her head against the wood interior. The hardness and discomfort of her position should have kept her awake, but she must have dozed because before she knew it, the driver was opening the door in front of Nick's townhouse—she supposed it was also hers, but that gave her no joy. She would contemplate the fact that she was mistress of this house when Nick was awake and in better form.

Right now, nothing in their situation felt right.

"We have arrived, Mrs. Riley," the doctor said.

Amelia rubbed her eyes, trying to clear the tiredness. "Try the knocker on the door," she instructed. "Let whoever answers know assistance is needed."

The driver did as asked, and Amelia pushed herself up to a sitting position, the doctor checking Nick's head and shaking his own head. Nick leaned heavily against her like a dead weight.

Amelia spied half the household coming down the stairs and around the side of the townhouse. The doctor stepped out of the carriage and met with the man that had once treated Amelia for her twisted ankle.

"Be careful when you move him; he's not been stitched up just yet. We need to make sure the bullet fragments are out."

"Oh, miss," Mrs. Coleman, the housekeeper, said as she climbed into the carriage to help lift Nick from where he rested against Amelia. The housekeeper placed her hand against Amelia's cheek. "You're soaked right through. Let's get both of you inside and get you dry and warm."

Mrs. Coleman gave Amelia's hand a squeeze of reassurance. Amelia wasn't sure what set her off, but she sucked in a breath as her lips started to tremble and her eyes filled with tears. She could not break down now. She needed to remain strong.

"Did you get my post?" Amelia asked, blinking away her tears of gratitude.

"More than an hour ago. We've been fretting over Mr. Riley's welfare. Huxley came home last night; wanted to ensure we had the doctor here waiting for him."

"Is Huxley here?"

"Left this morning; haven't heard from him since."

Liam, the footman, ducked his head into the carriage. "Where's his injuries? I want to avoid them if I can."

"His right shoulder," Amelia answered, knowing neither would see the bandage under Nick's shirt. They hadn't taken the risk of putting on his jacket. The fewer clothes he wore right now, the better they could get to his bullet wound, should it start bleeding again.

Liam climbed in, making the interior of the carriage smaller by the second. "Slide on out, Miss Gr—Mrs. Riley. I'll turn him around and take his weight. Mrs. Coleman can take his legs with Cook's help."

She did as she was asked and watched Joshua, who was the cook, climb in to where she'd been sitting.

Amelia started to shiver when a gust of wind whipped up against her. It was no warmer in the middle of the city than it had been in Highgate. She pinched her lips closed to keep her teeth from chattering and backed up toward the stairs, wrapping her arms around herself, trying to warm up with the friction of her hands rubbing over her chilled body.

She didn't go into the house until Nick was carried up the stairs.

"Doctor, I wish we were seeing each other again under different circumstances," she said to the man who walked up the stairs with her.

"I hear his fever has not yet abated," the doctor said.

"It hasn't. I'm afraid for him."

"Let me take a look at the wound before you worry yourself further."

"How can you remain so calm?" she asked.

"It's what I do, Mrs. Riley. I promise to do everything within my power to aid your husband. He's in good hands here. I have colleagues standing by, should their expertise or assistance be required."

At the doctor's assertion, Amelia took the first breath of relief she'd taken since finding her husband in his current state.

"Your reassurance goes a long way in settling my nerves," she admitted.

He took her arm, leading her inside, and the staff looked at her and the doctor for direction.

Amelia didn't take time to think; she acted, running up the stairs ahead of everyone, leading the way. "He needs to be set up in his room," she shouted down at them. "Mrs. Coleman, will you get some cold water and linens? We need to bring down his fever; he's been burning up since early morning and it's doing him no favors."

"Right away, Mrs. Riley."

"Jenny," Amelia said to one of the maids who had followed her up the stairs, "bring up some strong spirits. Whiskey, bourbon—it doesn't matter as long as it's strong enough to burn away any infection we note when we change his bandages." The doctor was at her shoulder, silently abiding by her direction. "Is there anything I missed?"

"Nothing. We need to look at the wound before we can make any other plans."

They all made haste, understanding their employer's dire condition. Amelia threw open Nick's bedroom door and rushed toward the bed so she could toss the blankets and sheets to the foot. As Liam and Joshua set Nick on the bed, she saw the first sign of life from him in more than a day and nearly screamed in excitement at the development. He rolled his good shoulder, stretching it as he slept, and turned his head to the side.

Amelia exhaled in a rush. Had she been holding her breath, waiting for that exact thing to happen? She thought she might have been, and the relief that filled her gave her extra hope and determination to see Nick well as soon as they could manage it. But she supposed a lot depended upon him. She would just have to give him reason to come back to her...and the waking world.

"Nick?" she said softly, hoping his eyes would open so she could talk to him again, see the smoldering gray that always filled his gaze and looked upon her with nothing short of need.

She looked away, saddened by the fact that he didn't stir. That didn't mean she would give up on him. He'd always been there for her, and she wouldn't hesitate to do the same.

Amelia placed her hand to his forehead and was disappointed that sweat beaded on his brow.

"His fever is worsening." The starkness of her own words sliced a streak of fear though her bones. "Doctor, will you help me remove his clothes?"

The doctor was already standing there, scissors in hand. "Probably better to cut his shirt off."

Amelia nodded and let the doctor take over, doing everything he asked her. He washed away the yarrow that filled Nick's wound and pressed the skin to test the coloring.

"The fever is doing its job," he said.

"And what precisely is that?"

"Fighting any infection. The wound is in good shape and ready to be stitched."

"Can we not pack it with more of the herb?"

"Can't risk it," the doctor said, opening his bag of instruments and pulling out thick thread and a needle.

Amelia took a calming breath. It was part relief, part dread she felt. But with the doctor here, she could almost see the light around the corner.

Nick heard his name through the darkness, like a beacon attempting to draw him nearer. It was faint, but it was there. His focus was on the dream before him, reenacting a scene that was full of sick depravity. Not the worst of his memories but the only one to etch a physical memento on his body.

His hands were bound, unable to move and protect the rest of his body. Cold air licked across his skin, as chilly as frost on a winter's morning. He was already tired, having fought against being tied up in the first place. He was sure his shoulder was dislocated, as it wasn't working properly and seemed to throb with an ache so painful it made him want to throw up.

There were no fewer than two broken noses and three cracked ribs among the vicar's followers. He'd never been happier that he'd been bigger than the rest of the children in the school. How else would he have defended himself? No one else had stood up for him or tried to stop the vicar. They'd held Nick down, forcing him into compliance. Nick would have none of it.

"Nick." The voice he'd heard earlier was closer now, repeating his name over and over again. It was familiar, and he wanted to go toward it.

He turned back to the scene so clear in his memories, which seemed impossible, because how could he see himself this way when he'd been the one bound, not the onlooker by any means? There had been so many onlookers. They were all as guilty as the man who had wielded the whip.

The first lash of many fell hard and cutting against his back. The sound repulsed him. He couldn't use a riding whip when they were given the opportunity to ride on horseback. He refused to hurt an animal helpless to his whims. The same rule did not apply to the vicar. He was a cruel man. Bent on a path of destruction. Filled with so much hate, Nick was sure the man's soul was black as pitch.

The demon who delivered the blow hid in shadows, but Nick knew the man from memory. Nick knew upon whom he needed to exact his revenge to stop these dreams. To keep away the memories that haunted him.

"Tell me, boy—who is your master?"

"No one," his younger self replied.

Snap.

"*Repeat after me if you want to walk away from this,*" the devil said.

"*You will not own me. No one will.*"

A lesson his mother had taught him. While her trade was sex, she was not a victim of the whims of men. Nick would not be a victim and give in to the man who wanted to own him.

"*Willfulness is the devil's work upon you. I will beat it out of you if I must.*"

Snap.

Nick was no longer standing, his wrists pulled against the ropes; he was limp, weakly held in place only by the rope that restrained him.

The whip cut raw welt after raw welt into his back. Yet Nick refused to give the vicar what he wanted.

"*I will break you, boy.*"

"Fuck you," Nick said in response, spitting on the floor.

He wiped away the remaining spittle against his bare arm. There was blood on his mouth, probably from biting his tongue the last time the lash fell against him. But he didn't care. He would do this until he was dead before he would give in.

Snap. Crack. Snap.

The painful strokes came in quick succession.

Nick lost track of how many times the leathers fell against his back. Hot, scalding pain burned through him with every hit. Liquid ran over the back of his bare legs, tickling toward the front like warm fingers defiling his skin.

He couldn't get his feet under him anymore. He just prayed the vicar's arm tired before he lost more blood than he could afford. Before he lost his ability to stay lucid and the vicar tried to *take him, like he had the other boys, like he had watched the vicar take his friend, Michael Shauley.*

"What have you to say now, demon child?"

"I cannot be broken." Though his voice certainly was. "You will have to hit me harder," he said spitefully.

Nick probably shouldn't have said that, but the more he thought about the fate that awaited him if he gave in, the more he wanted to kill the vicar with his own two hands. He remained strong and finally got one foot under him and pushed himself up so he wasn't hanging by the rope. The feeling tingled back into his arms, and the throbbing at his shoulder intensified.

"Nick!" called the lyrical voice again, drawing him away from the bloody scene that kept repeating and that he seemed trapped to relive over and over again.

He wanted to go toward the voice. He needed to pull himself away from the nightmare he watched unfold for so many nights now that he wondered if he imagined it in the first place. He tried to reach behind him to touch the scars on his back, but his hands wouldn't move. Was he bound even now?

He struggled against the restraints, growing more panicked by the minute. It was like he was both part of and a witness to his past.

He couldn't escape it.

He'd never been able to run far from it. His dreams wouldn't free him. They bound him as sure as the rope had bound his body to the whipping post.

"Nick."

Louder this time.

Closer.

He wanted to reach out and touch the sound that echoed around him, that was the only thing drawing him out of the darkness.

The coolness of the room made him shiver; his teeth chattered. Softness brushed against his skin. Not like the trickle of blood that had run over his broken body; this was different, soothing, kind. Like hands covering him all over at once, warming him, urging him away from the darkness he was helpless but to stare into.

He didn't want to leave the past. He wasn't ready to make that change. He could not forget those he must repay for their sins.

Crack.

Nick's body swayed limp beneath his restraints once again. His body was broken, bleeding. The pain was unbearable as his feet tried and tried again to get under him, to lift him up, to give him the strength he needed to get through this. But the blood on the floor made it impossible to find steady ground.

What did this memory hold that was so important he couldn't let it go?

His past was inescapable. It existed just like this in his memories.

Why did he want to stay here?

To remember. To destroy the man who had done this to him and so many others. He needed to always remember where he came from. Remember the faces of those against whom he sought revenge.

"You can't leave me like this," a sorrowful voice whispered in his ear.

He didn't want that voice to be sad. And that was when he realized he didn't want to be trapped in this reality anymore.

Nick opened his eyes, squinting at first as he pulled himself out of the somnambulant state in which he was trapped. The simultaneous itch and burn in his arm had him twisting, trying to get comfortable where he lay. He tried to raise his forearm to block the sun from his eyes, but it didn't move. He shielded out the harsh light of day with his other hand.

"Nick! Thank God." Amelia's voice was like a thousand shards of glass crashing around him, and he flinched. His eyes squeezed shut to put him back in darkness. His vision wavered, even as he tried to blink them open again.

"Sorry," she said in a much quieter tone. "Here. Drink this."

A spoon parted his lips, allowing water to slide over his dry tongue. He took every drop greedily, rolling it around to hydrate him. He was so thirsty it was like he hadn't had a drink in a year.

Nick blinked a few more times until his eyes came into focus, and he was staring at the canopy of his bed in London. They'd been in Highgate. Why weren't they in Highgate now? He needed to be there to exact his revenge. Then he recalled his last moments of lucidity. He'd been shot. He had to find Shauley and kill the bastard. The list of men who would be repaid for their misdeeds was ever growing.

"How long have we been here?" Nick asked, his voice groggy and sounding not like his own.

"Two days. I had to bring you home to be treated by your doctor. You grew feverish…Nick, you scared me half to death…I can't tell you how glad I am to see you awake. It means you're on the mend."

Her words were rapid, as though she had a million things she needed to tell him all at once. But he could barely comprehend all that she said. Still unable to move his tongue around, he let her fill the silence with her chatter. Her voice had a musical quality to it. One to which he could fall asleep.

She squeezed his hand and placed the spoon up to his mouth again. "Don't you dare fall back to sleep. Try to stay awake, darling. The doctor will want to examine you."

With his good hand he reached for the arm that burned. It was held tight to his body by linens tying it in place, keeping it stationary. When his fingers prodded his shoulder he hissed in a pained breath and dropped his good arm to the bed. It fell like a dead weight, and Nick hated nothing more than being weak and helpless to defend himself.

"I had to keep your arm steady," she said apologetically. "Your nightmares grew worse over the last day. You were struggling and moving around so much I thought you'd tear all your stitches."

He could imagine.

"Huxley?"

"A missive arrived from him an hour ago. He said he would be back in London before the dinner hour. That's the first I've heard from him since you were found in the courtyard of the inn. No one knows how you got there, Nick. Do you remember what happened?"

"Shauley." His tongue stuck to the roof of his mouth; the name came out garbled.

As Amelia came closer, the mattress dipped by his hip. "Let me help you sit up so you can take a glass of water. It will help you talk. But you don't have to say anything yet if you don't want to. All that matters is that we are home, and you are going to be all right. I was so afraid, Nick. God, I was so afraid you were lost to me."

Gingerly, Amelia slid her arm behind his back and pulled him up enough that she could prop him up with a few pillows. Nick rotated his aching shoulder, feeling the pain that rushed through his arm with the movement. Pain meant he was alive. Pain meant he was on the mend and could find the strength to track down Shauley once and for all.

"Be careful with your movements. We had to stitch the wound, and you might pull the stitches loose if you aren't careful."

A cool glass pressed to his lips and water washed over his tongue. He drank it down, taking the glass from her with his good hand before he was finished and handing it back to her when it was empty.

He would not be treated as an invalid, not even by his pretty wife.

Cracking his eyes open, he found the light still bothered him, but the pain in his head had lessened. "Can you draw the curtains?" he asked.

"Of course." She scrambled off the bed and yanked the heavy brocade material closed, blanketing the room in shadows. When he opened his eyes again, he was able to focus on his room and on his wife. Amelia approached the bed with tentative steps, sat on the edge of the mattress, and placed a hand over his forearm where it rested across his abdomen.

Amelia's hair was down and braided to one side. Dark circles were visible beneath her eyes, as though she hadn't slept in days. He reached out and placed his hand against her cheek. She nuzzled into him with a soft sigh. "I've missed you beyond expression. I've missed you so much, Nick."

"I'm sorry to have distressed you. I have caused you pain, and that's not something I take lightly."

"You have nothing to apologize for, just...just let me take care of you. The doctor said it would be a few weeks before you were back to your old self. I almost didn't believe you would come out of your fever, and when you didn't wake after that, I thought you were lost to me."

"Never lost. I could hear you calling my name. I wanted to come back to you with every whispered word."

Amelia stood and kissed his forehead as one might a sick child. He grabbed hold of her arm so she couldn't escape him again. "Don't leave. Not yet."

"I have to call for the doctor."

"The doctor can wait."

"Nick." There was admonishment in the way she said his name.

"Sit with me. We have things to discuss before the doctor interrupts us. I have all these holes in my memory I need to fill. To understand what happened."

She gingerly sat on the edge of the bed again, the back of her hand pressed to his forehead, checking his temperature.

With a heavy sigh, she said, "I will humor you for a while. But my instructions were to call on the doctor immediately."

"In Highgate, who found me?" he asked.

"The innkeeper. But news went around the village shortly after you made your way to the inn courtyard. Everyone wanted to know what had happened, if you were alive."

Amelia took an audibly unsteady breath before she could continue. "The fear that paralyzed me when I saw you…"

Sitting so close, he could see that her eyes were bloodshot, tired. Had she stayed awake these past few days?

"Have you left this room at all?" he asked.

"I couldn't. I wanted to be here in case you woke. Don't ask me to leave now; this is my room too."

"I want you here, Amelia." Nick pulled her closer with his good arm, her head pressed against his bicep. He brushed her hair away from her temple and ran his fingers through the soft brown tresses. "This is no way to spend our honeymoon. When I'm better, I will take you wherever you want."

"I don't want to go anywhere. I want you well again. All that matters is that I am wherever you are."

"I promise not to go anywhere without you."

She lifted her head and gave him a curious look, with one eyebrow raised. "I will never forgive myself for not following you that morning. There were things left unsaid. Things I should have told you."

"And have me risk your safety? Not as long as there is breath in me would I even consider such a thing, Amelia. Had you been hurt in place of me, I would never be able to live with myself."

She exhaled and touched the scruff on the side of his face, her expression patient and tender. "The household has been eager for your recovery. I don't think we should keep them waiting much longer." She moved away from him.

It was more than he could take at present. "Amelia."

She turned back to him. "I'm just going to get fresh linens. We'll have to put new bandages on you before I help you dress."

He was in no shape to argue, so he wisely let her go about her tasks, watching the sway of her hips with each gentle move of her body around his room. She looked at home in here as she found what she needed.

She was an image that stole his breath away.

When she returned to his side and started to loosen the knot holding his arm crossed over his body, he could smell the faint scent of lilacs in her hair. He leaned forward, inhaling deeper.

"Nick?"

"You smell good enough to eat."

She chuckled softly. "You're in no shape for such activities. Besides, Joshua has made all sorts of dishes for you, hoping you would wake and be famished enough to eat a whole meal. He's been cooking your favorite foods for two days straight."

Nick nuzzled his nose close to her ear. His lips brushed the shell, but he didn't kiss her. He did need to eat proper food, something to get the pasty taste out of his mouth. Until he felt steady enough to remain awake, he would leave his wife alone.

Amelia's fingers stilled; she cleared her throat. Nick watched her pulse flutter and her chest rise with each inhalation. It seemed all sorts of appetites were upon him now that he was awake, and his body stirred in reaction to her close proximity.

"We'll start you on broth," she said, pulling the soiled linen away from his arm.

Nick hissed in a pained breath that doused every one of his desires. "Shit. That's more painful than I thought it would be."

"We had to dig the bullet out; it was lodged against the bone."

"Shauley aimed to injure, not kill me."

Amelia pulled away from him, her eyes narrowed. "What do you mean?"

"He wanted to make a move against the vicar before I did, so he just made sure I was down and out of the race."

She seemed perplexed by this revelation and thought it over before saying, "I need to tell you something, Nick."

Amelia worried her bottom lip as she focused on his arm and carefully removed the bits of gauze that stuck to his shoulder. He glanced down at the wound that had scabbed around the black stitches holding the center of the hole closed. He'd had so many injuries over the years, from his fighting days mostly, that the sight didn't put him off. He would have prodded at it to see just how sensitive it was, but Amelia seemed a little sick to her stomach, looking at the wound.

"You gave us all a fright when your fever set in the day after we pulled out the bullet. We all thought the doctor was going to have to open you back up and see if a piece of metal had been left behind." She used a damp towel to clean around the wound, wiping away the dried blood that had crusted along his arm.

"What was it you needed to tell me?"

"It's about Shauley. I saw him…"

Nick pushed himself into a sitting position, ready to get dressed, find a horse, and chase down the bastard.

Amelia pressed her hand against his chest forcing him to focus on her. "I saw him before you had your run-in with him. He was different. Like his anger was gone; actually, more like it never existed toward me. I couldn't figure out why he'd had a change of heart, why he didn't try to hurt me. I didn't know what to make of my conversation with him. I should have told you."

"Why didn't you?"

"I will never forgive myself for the idiocy of not telling you. After almost having lost you...I hate myself for that lie, even if it was one of omission."

Nick grabbed her hand. "None of this is your fault."

She shook her head, not listening to him. "It was the first day we fought. You stormed out of our room. I should have followed; instead, I wanted to wallow a while in my anger. I didn't tell you about Shauley because he let me go. I thought he was going to kill me once and for all when he had a second chance. But he let me go...on a promise."

"What did you promise him?"

"That I would convince you to leave Highgate."

"Is that why you brought me back to London? To fulfill your promise to him?" Even if she had done it for that purpose, Nick couldn't find it in him to be angry. Not after what she must have felt while he lay dead to the world, keeping company with his nightmares.

"Only your need to see a doctor with more expertise than the healer drew me here. I was afraid to move you. Afraid you would be lost to us and was dredging up a thousand reasons why the carriage ride would kill you. But the healer and doctor assured me that we had to come home. And we did. There were medicines here your physician had to administer. And he was better suited to handle your wound than the healer."

"The healer?" Nick laughed, but it was cut short by the pain it caused him.

"Yes, the woman you commissioned for my veil. She was a midwife before she became a seamstress." Amelia tipped up her chin, leaning in close to look at the stitches on his shoulder and pressing a cloth against them. "You mustn't move about so much. Let's bandage you up and call for the doctor now."

He nodded and let her go about tending him. Her touch was careful and gentle as she applied an ointment that smelled of lavender to the cut before covering it. He watched in silent regard until she needed his assistance in putting on his shirt.

"I don't think I've ever not been able to dress myself."

"Not even after one of your fights?"

"Not even. Dislocated bones are easily reset. Broken ones just need a good splint. We both know blood washes away. The only thing to cure the rage after one of my fights was a good woman."

She turned away, a frown on her face.

That had been the wrong thing to say. But dammit, he felt like shit, was sure he smelled just as bad, and all he could think about was his wife, naked and ready for him. And worse, he knew he didn't have the strength at present to fulfill either of their needs properly.

That didn't stop him from watching her; hell, he couldn't take his eyes off her.

"What do we do now, Nick?"

"We find Shauley and the vicar."

"The monk—John…was he the one who watched it all transpire when you were a boy?"

Nick nodded, not able to voice what had happened all those years ago.

"And I told you where to find him as though he were a friend who could help."

"It is far from your doing. And it led me to Shauley, which means I know where to find him."

"Shauley was there, with the monk?" A furrow formed between her eyes.

He nodded affirmatively. "They knew each other. And while the monk pretended not to recognize or remember me, he knew exactly who Shauley was."

"Is Shauley protecting the vicar? I don't understand why he would do that. His fate was the same as yours. What man would grow to accept that?"

"Your guess is as good as mine, but I don't believe he is protecting them. I'm missing a bigger part of the picture; I just haven't figured out what it is."

"Nick, when he found me in the field, he said I needed to get you away. He had things to take care of and that you were interfering. It makes sense that he has the same goal in mind as you."

Nick hated to be in line with an enemy. "Even if he wants the same outcome for the vicar, it does not erase what Shauley did to you."

Nick swung his legs over the side of the bed. His head bowed as he breathed through the pain that infiltrated his body so forcefully that his head spun and his vision went black for a moment.

"I know that better than anyone. He needs to be tried for his crimes. Justice must be sought for those he hurt in his pursuit of this mad revenge he concocted. While my brother was not an innocent man, he deserved a better chance. Shauley all but admitted to being a part of my brother's murder."

"I suspected but didn't know for sure, so I said nothing. Our secrets have dug us into a hole. I know I haven't been forthcoming with you and because of that, we are where we are today. Everything that has happened is my own fault."

"I think we can both agree that it's neither of our fault." Her hand rested on his arm. "Please, stay in bed a while longer. Your body is trying to heal from the ordeal."

Weakness was not an option. He inhaled deeply and concentrated on the even tone of his heartbeat. It was a simple tactic he always used before a fighting match, one that centered and grounded him to the moment. The dizziness subsided as he rolled his head around his shoulders.

This was no different from getting up after a bad beating. He always persevered, no matter the odds against him. He ignored the sting of his shoulder and focused on what needed to be done. He stood and nearly fell over but caught himself by grabbing the post of the bed.

Amelia rushed forward to catch him under the arm. "What do you think you're doing?"

Did she honestly believe she could take his weight? He took a careful step forward. He was only wearing smalls and a shirt, and needed to pull on a pair of trousers before he could go anywhere. But Amelia led him away from the dressing room and toward the plunge bath.

"I have to deal with Shauley," he said in protest.

"If you think I'll let you leave this house in your current state—"

"I'm not asking, Amelia. This is happening. I won't make you stay here, wondering what else I've gotten myself into. You can come back to Highgate with me. We can end this together."

She didn't say anything as she helped him over to the porcelain washstand. Nick braced himself over the counter and looked at himself in the mirror. He'd definitely seen better days, but he'd never been shot before, and considering he'd lost two days to fever…he was ready to take on the world, if that was what was required of him. Thank God it wasn't as dire as that.

Shauley would be a dead man when he caught up to him. The vicar and his disciples would fare no better. And by Amelia's nonanswer, he assumed she would be right there by his side. Things were definitely looking up.

Amelia turned on the tap behind him. "You are not going anywhere without a long soak in the tub. I'll make sure your shoulder stays dry."

Nick rinsed his mouth out, swished some of the paste around to get rid of the taste left behind from two days of sleep and no food. Odd that he wasn't hungry. He spied his wife leaning over the bath, testing the temperature of the water. Her hair fell forward, skimming the surface. He might not be hungry for food, but there were other appetites that could be sated. He scratched the side of his face. His beard was in desperate need of trimming.

"I'd prefer you focused your attentions elsewhere than on my shoulder."

Her hand stopped moving above the water, and her head turned to the side so she could look at him. "Is that so?"

"Give me one reason we shouldn't indulge our other appetites."

Amelia dried off her hand on the towel draped over the tub and left the water running; it was only a quarter of the way full.

"You need to rest and avoid all strain."

"That's for the doctor to tell me, isn't it?"

"You don't think I have your best interests in mind?" He did, but her voice was breathless as she said it.

"I think we are missing out on a fantastic honeymoon. I have a few days of neglect to catch up for."

"Hardly, Nick. What you need is to heal. Healing takes time."

"Help me out of my clothes, won't you?"

She looked down, a frown still clear on her face. Did she see the evidence of his desire?

"I was hoping for more enthusiasm than that," he said.

"Nick you are on the mend, and in no shape for...for marital affairs." Her blushing was the most beautiful thing.

"I think we need to make sure everything is in working order. I've gone through quite the ordeal."

"If you think I'll believe that excuse, you're sadly mistaken. The doctor ordered rest."

"How about I let you have complete control. I know how much you like ordering me about when it involves intimacy." He traced his finger down the side of her arm. She didn't stop him by the time he'd reached the bend of her elbow, and her lips parted ever so slightly. He took that as an invitation to lower his mouth, pressing his lips against hers.

He was careful, gentle. He didn't want her to stop what he had started. Sore and tired were perfect descriptions for what he felt, but under all that was the need to feel his wife. Her life, her vivacity.

Her hand curled around his bad arm, causing him to hiss in a breath.

She pulled away, her eyes blinking away the fog of arousal in which he'd nearly drowned her better judgment. "I'm sorry. We should stop before things get out of hand." She stared at his arm, a cringe curling up her face.

"I prefer things being out of hand where you're concerned, Amelia."

He loosened the tie holding up his smalls. The material slid off his hips and pooled around his feet. Her gaze caught on his erection.

"Now I have your attention."

She sucked in her bottom lip as she looked up at him. "I don't want to hurt you, Nick."

"It'll be a good kind of hurt." He took her hand and stepped into the bath. He wasn't giving her the opportunity to escape.

He released the buttons that marched down the front of her dress from neck to stomach. She didn't protest; she helped by shrugging out of her clothes once they were loose and untied the more complicated bindings he couldn't get at with one hand.

"Don't make me regret this," she said in warning.

He gave her a sure smile. She wouldn't have cause to regret a single moment. His cock actually throbbed when she pulled her chemise over her head and let it flutter to the floor to land on the heap of her other clothes. She stepped into the water, her back to him as she shut off the flow of the tap. He pressed his erection against her backside, loving how the curve of her bottom felt against him. He ran his fingers down between her cheeks, pressing his thumb against the puckered hole of her rear. She froze, bent over and waiting.

"I want to fuck that sweet spot of you again, but I need more strength than I currently have."

She stood and turned. "You said I could be in charge."

"I did, didn't I?"

He gave her a lopsided grin as she helped him sit and stretch his legs out in the hot water. Her legs were on either side of his, her feet firmly planted next to his thighs. His hand reached up and cupped her mound. She was close enough that he could kiss her there, and he didn't wait for permission. Parting the lips of her sex, he revealed her hood-covered clitoris. He curled his arm around her hips and pulled her closer to his mouth and tasted the sweet juices of her cunt on his tongue with a groan.

"I can't stand like this much longer." She pulled away from his mouth, and he nearly grabbed her with his bad arm to keep her in place but thought better of it at the last moment.

She settled in the water around his thighs, hovering just above his straining cock. Before he could comment on her teasing ways, she was sinking down on his length. Head thrown back, her small hands curled around the edge of the bath. Once fully seated, she looked him straight in the eye. The steam from the room had a light sheen of water, adding shine to her skin. He kissed her chin. Her cheek, her nose, then lazily slid his tongue past her lips and sucked her tongue, slow and sweet.

She moved over him then, lifting herself in a mimic of their mouths. He didn't rush her; he wanted this to last as long as it took the water to cool.

He could tell the moment her senses heightened, for her pace quickened, and her breathing grew erratic. He lowered his hand between them and rubbed her clitoris, letting her get closer to her release. When he felt the first rippling of her orgasm tighten her sheath around him, like a fist pumping his cock, he drove up into her, sloshing water over the edge of the bath, onto the tiled floor. He didn't give a damn what kind of mess he made.

Amelia's whole body was trembling by the time he came. His orgasm had never felt so fucking good.

When his cock stopped twitching inside her, she gave him a sweet, closed-mouth kiss. When she pulled back, she asked, "Did I hurt you?"

"God, no. I could do that all day, Amelia. Sometimes I want to forget the world around us and just spend my every waking moment with you...inside you."

She rested her forehead against his and closed her eyes. His cock was still buried deep inside her, and he liked it that way; his cock hadn't lost its hardness, not in the least.

Nick kissed her collarbone, sliding his tongue across her skin and flexing his hips to start their lovemaking again.

She tangled one hand in the hair at the back of his head, her finger twirling out an unknown pattern, twisting strands of hair around them in the process. Amelia kissed him again on the lips, pulling away to say, "Let me pleasure you again, my insatiable husband."

And she did. They stayed in the water until they were both prunes and so wrung out from intercourse they could barely climb out.

CHAPTER ELEVEN

Amelia stared down at the ledger in front of her, not really reading what was there. The mantel clock ticked the seconds in the background, giving her something to focus on when her mind seemed to be everywhere and nowhere, all at the same time. She'd convinced Nick to stay in London for the remainder of the week. It wasn't nearly enough time for him to heal, but it allowed him to get his strength up.

The doctor had been impressed that Nick was able to move around and had ensured Amelia it was a sign that he would heal quickly, now that the fever had passed. That didn't give Nick free rein to carry on in his usual fashion, however. It would take time to get to that point. And Nick proved to be everything but patient in this matter.

The house was eerily silent, except for the damn clock that was friend and foe all at once. She'd come down to the study early, knowing she needed to leave before Nick woke. Despite what he might think, he did need to relax and not strain himself. Those were the doctor's orders, and she was trying desperately to abide by them.

No one had come upstairs to the study all morning. It was closing in on the lunch hour, and her stomach growled after having missed breakfast. It was odd, but she couldn't bring herself to go down to the kitchen to face everyone's scrutiny quite yet. She'd been under the mantle of wife and healer these past few days and didn't know how to talk to the people she'd befriended while working here.

The questions they must have. About Nick and about their marriage. About how this affected the household. Well, she had to face them sooner or later.

The only thing that worried her was that they might treat her differently now that she was the mistress of the house. She didn't want to be treated differently. She'd grown close to everyone here. They'd championed her and come together to support her after her brother had tried to haul her away with force. They'd plied her with tea and given her comfort after news of her brother's death surfaced. They'd welcomed her with open arms, treating her like one of them.

And damn it, she was one of them! That would not change.

She focused on the blurred numbers and words of the ledger. She wasn't sure why she bothered. Her mind was elsewhere. Focused on Nick, to be precise.

Could she face Shauley again? She wasn't sure. And she wasn't afraid for herself but for what Shauley might do to her husband. What if he decided to kill Nick this time?

Slamming the book shut with a growl of frustration, she pushed away from her desk. She walked down to the kitchen without further ado. It was time to get this over with.

Huxley wasn't present in the dining hall, but she knew he had to be somewhere; he'd arrived home last night and had spoken with Nick at length. She'd remained for some of the conversation, learning what Huxley had been up to in his absence, but she'd left them for a spell to discuss any other private matters.

Since she was too early for lunch, Amelia headed toward the housekeeper's office in search of Mrs. Coleman. She faced the wooden paneled door and took a deep breath. Before she could talk herself out of doing what she'd worked up the courage to do, Amelia gave the door a light rap with her knuckles.

Mrs. Coleman swung the door open.

"Good afternoon, Mrs. Coleman." Amelia folded her hands in front of her.

"Good day, child. Did you need me?"

"I wanted to talk about what happened in Highgate."

"We had word before you were even married. Wanted to go, we did, but Mr. Riley said it was to be a small affair."

Smallish, she thought. The village folk probably hadn't given Nick much say. Amelia raised her eyebrows, surprised Mrs. Coleman had guessed her reasons for being here. "I meant to discuss it with you earlier. My only concern on arriving home was to help Nick heal, and I feel awful for not coming down sooner to address everyone."

"You needn't worry. Huxley delivered the news, and none of us could be happier."

"No one believes I have other reasons for trapping him in marriage?"

"You couldn't force Mr. Riley to do anything he didn't want to do in the end. And I'm not likely to judge you, considering my own past. No one would take on a pregnant woman without a husband to work in a fine house such as this. I understand what desire does to a person, Mrs. Riley. You found yourself a good man, one who won't leave you when things don't go the way they should."

Amelia's mouth flapped. How was she supposed to respond to that? "Perhaps I should clarify that I am not with child."

"And I wasn't suggesting *that*. Just that you two weren't hiding the fact that you've shared a room almost as long as you have been here."

Amelia couldn't help the blush that heated her face.

While she suspected the household knew exactly what was happening behind closed doors, hearing it as bluntly as that was another thing entirely.

"I don't want anything to change, Mrs. Coleman. I am Nick's wife but also his secretary. I'm…I'm a friend to everyone in this house."

"I should hope so." The housekeeper stood from her chair and pocketed her keys. She ushered Amelia out of her office. "Let's see if Joshua needs assistance bringing lunch into the dining hall, Mrs. Riley. We don't expect you to eat down here with us, as you'll be supping with Mr. Riley when he's on his feet again. But we would like your company for as long as we can have it."

Amelia didn't argue with Mrs. Coleman. A smile lit up her whole face, and the tension she initially had felt in facing the staff was vanquished.

Happiness was a precious thing she would never take for granted. This was her home. And without the people who made up this household, she could never be whole. And without Nick, she knew she was nothing. They all—their little band of misfits and miscreants—made each other.

"I can hardly believe you married your mistress, Nick. It's not something for which society will forgive you. If you want to mingle in their circles, you have to play by their rules." Nick watched his friend and former mistress, Victoria, drum her nails along the edge of her tea saucer, clearly irritated by his actions. She'd come to visit him after hearing he'd woken from his fever. It seemed the whole city waited with bated breath for him to come out of the sleep that had held him.

"Amelia was never my mistress," he clarified, though he shouldn't have to do any such thing.

Victoria was shaking her head, not listening to him. "It's simply not done."

Had it really only been a few weeks ago that he'd sat last with his friend Victoria? He'd had tea, and they had argued about Amelia. The women were determined to dislike each other on merit alone. He understood their differences, considering Victoria had once shared his bed. But Amelia was the only woman ever to work her way into his heart. And he needed them to get on amicably, as they were each an important part of his life.

"We've been friends long enough that I hope you can put aside your differences with Amelia."

Nick shifted in his chair, trying to focus on anything but the pain that shot through his shoulder and arm. He'd been pushing himself since he woke yesterday. He couldn't help it;

he needed to be strong. More than that, he needed to be able to go after Shauley and finish what they had started.

"Do you realize the scandal this has created, Nick?" Victoria pattered on. "You might not want to call her your mistress, but she is your acting secretary. It undermines you to marry someone beneath you like that. With your wealth and your status in society, you could have married into a prominent family."

And that was the last thing he ever wanted.

While Nick might have been considered a sought-after bachelor for his worth alone, mothers and chaperones of eligible young ladies often shied away and kept their distance, exactly where he liked them. He had never wanted to buy his way into society, nor did he want to mingle with the vapid daughters of dukes and marquesses.

"I wasn't asking your opinion on the matter, Victoria."

Nick impatiently tapped his hand over his knee. He'd known this would be her reaction, yet he'd entertained the idea of seeing her this afternoon after she'd sent a card.

Nick never imagined he would be a husband. Amelia had changed him. He liked the person he was when he was with her. He liked what she represented.

Home.

"I'm giving my opinion freely," she shot back, dropping a cube of sugar in her tea and stirring it around.

"Your view doesn't change the fact that I'm married, whether you approve of Amelia or not."

"I'm surprised you would pick someone about whom you know so little over me."

Nick frowned and stared into his coffee cup. Surely she didn't mean that. "You know we wouldn't have suited."

"Perhaps," she agreed, though it didn't seem convincing. "But that doesn't negate the fact that you've known Miss Grant less than a month."

"Mrs. Riley," he corrected his friend. "You will respectfully address my wife as Mrs. Riley. If you cannot accept that, perhaps we should cut our ties now."

Victoria inhaled sharply. "How dare you choose her over me."

"She is my wife."

"And what does she know about you? Have you told her where you come from? How you grew up? Can she accept you for the man you really are?"

Before Victoria could say more, he firmly said, "She knows everything."

There could be no more secrets between them. And there would be no hiding his past forever when he finally got his revenge on the man who'd taken his childhood from him.

Victoria eyed him coolly over her tea before taking a sip. "I've never known you to trust anyone so easily."

There had been nothing easy about his relationship with Amelia. But that wasn't for Victoria to know. Frankly, none of it was any of her damn business.

"Then maybe the questions you need to ask are why I trust her as much as I do. Why I married her when I never had the desire to marry before. Jealousy has never looked good on you, Vic, yet you insist on that state where Amelia is concerned. You and I were friends long before we were lovers, and you wear pettiness as poorly as you wear jealousy. Have you forgotten what it's like to be my friend?"

She reached her hand out to touch his hand, but he pulled it away before she could; as much as the motion pained his shoulder, he didn't regret the decision of setting a physical boundary between them. He would give her no reason to think he was on the fence as a married man.

Victoria's brows scrunched and her eyes narrowed. "I have no reason to like her."

"I'm not asking you to like her. I'm asking you, as my *friend*, to understand why I chose her. And in time, you will like her."

Victoria pinched her lips together and turned her focus to the paintings in the room.

"I've known you a long time, Vic. Our friendship doesn't end because I found someone in my life to love."

Her eyes snapped to his, and she gave him a sad look. "I've never heard you say *that* before."

"Then take it to mean I'm true about my feelings. You're the only person to whom I can speak openly about this."

"Considering you were still sleeping in my bed only a week before you met her…"

Nick raised his hand. They had made headway; her trying to persuade him otherwise would get them nowhere. And their affair was a thing of the past.

"It was what it was, Vic. But what we had was over long before we were ready to admit it."

"How can you paint what we had with such a fine stroke?"

"Because the matter is that simple."

Victoria looked away from him with a miffed huff. "I can't promise I will ever warm to Amelia."

Nick smiled at his friend. He knew this wasn't easy for her to digest. "You will."

Victoria rolled her eyes. "If you insist."

Nick leaned back against the cushion, trying to find a comfortable position. "Now that I have you here, I need your help with one other thing," he said.

"I'm all out of wedding dresses," she teased.

Nick shook his head and put up his feet, as that seemed to help him achieve a better position in which to repose. He explained what he had in mind. He and Amelia had come a long way, and they'd had little time to celebrate the joyous occasion of their marriage. And there was something special he wanted to do for her.

"I want one thing to be clear, Nick. I'm doing this for you," Victoria said, agreeing.

He could accept that.

"Now tell me the whole story of what happened with your shoulder."

Nick did, leaving out no details, as Victoria knew nearly as much as Amelia about his sordid past with the vicarage school and Shauley. Nearly, but not all. He edited out the parts about his nightmares, about finding the vicar and losing him when he'd been so close to his goal.

"Where do you think Shauley is now?"

Nick shook his head. "I have no way of knowing. I do know he's no longer in Highgate. Huxley confirmed that."

Huxley had also been by the cabin, and Brother John still resided there, which surprised Nick. He thought the old man would have up and left after their last encounter. Huxley had not been able to ascertain whether the vicar was still residing with Brother John. But that was something Nick would find out on his own.

The door opened, and Amelia entered. "Oh, I didn't mean to interrupt." She turned to leave just as fast as she'd arrived.

"Don't go," Nick called out after her. "Join us. We were just discussing Shauley." He held out his hand, hoping she'd take that as a clear indication that he genuinely wanted her here. He wanted his wife by his side, not Victoria, and the sooner Victoria realized that, the sooner she would move on and accept what Amelia meant to him.

Amelia seemed reluctant, standing at the threshold of the door, looking beyond the parlor and then looking at him. Her indecision was clear, but she held her head high and came into the parlor, taking Nick's hand as she sat beside him on the sofa.

"When I heard Nick was awake, I had to stop in," Victoria said, standing. "I was so thankful to hear he had pulled through the ordeal. For now, I have a hundred things I need to take care of. I will stop in again soon, Nick."

Amelia stood when Victoria did. "I can see you out."

"I can find my way." Victoria slapped her gloves in her hand. "I suppose felicitations are in order, Mrs. Riley. I wish you two a prosperous marriage."

Nick grinned. Of course she wouldn't wish them one filled with love, laughter, and a healthy family.

"Thank you for stopping in, Miss Newgate," Amelia said, not bothering to reach out and take Victoria's hand, as friends might do.

Nick put his feet down and clumsily stood. The motion caused the stitching in his shoulder to pull. He ignored the twinge of pain and leaned into Amelia's side for support. Her arm went around his back, but she didn't act as though she was holding most of his weight against her.

Victoria inclined her head toward them both before leaving.

When his friend was gone, he pulled Amelia into his side, his hand firm at her hip. "Where have you been all morning?"

"Joshua was giving me instructions on baking a pie."

"A pie?"

"Mrs. Coleman insisted that keeping my hands busy would help ease my worries."

"Are you thinking of Shauley?"

"How could I not?"

Nick let Amelia go and fell back to the sofa. His breathing was slightly heavier than he would have liked. The effort to stand had been taxing.

"Nick. What have you done to yourself?"

"Strained my arm. I'll be fine."

Amelia tugged at his trousers, trying to free his shirt so she could get at the bandage on his shoulder.

"My lady, who knew you liked a man unable to do anything more than give his lovely wife verbal commands."

"Don't tease me, Nick. You've hurt yourself. I want to make sure you haven't opened up the stitches."

"I haven't. Stop fretting. If they didn't open yesterday in the bath, they won't open when I stand on my own."

"How can you be so sure?" She continued to pull up his shirt. Nick aided her where he could, but otherwise, he reserved his energy, knowing he'd need it for something more pleasurable if his wife wanted to strip him out of his clothes.

"I have pulled stitches before. I'm familiar with the ache associated with it. Everything is as it should be—I can promise you that—so stop worrying." He leaned back against the sofa. Her hands were like fluid magic wherever she touched his skin. "I love the way your hands feel on me."

She pulled them away, and Nick was forced to open his eyes and look at his confused wife.

"Why did you stop?"

"This is hardly an opportune time for this."

"Would you prefer I wait 'til I'm dead?" His words were bitter, crueler than he'd intended, but Amelia didn't seem perturbed by his tone.

"The same can be said in reverse." Her fingers trailed down his sternum and circled around his navel. "I will play along with whatever you need, as long as you don't pull your stitches."

Amelia's hand caressed the linen that covered his shoulder. He could barely feel her, and he wanted to feel the hard press of her hands along his body. He would never get enough of her, never stop craving her.

The thought of never being able to hold his wife in his arms had the ability to render him numb. So he would take all the feeling he could get, all the time.

"I'm impressed with how high your spirits are today; you seem more lively," Amelia mused, her fingers trailing up and down the buttons of his waistcoat, slipping them through their moorings painfully slow.

"The more I move about, the faster I'll heal."

"I'm going to guess that line of thinking comes from the days when you used to fight."

"It does. But it's nothing more than the truth. If you lay about hoping to get better, you won't. The sooner you carry on your normal activities, the easier it is to get back into the swing of daily life."

"Is that an excuse to get my undivided…carnal attention?"

"That might have something to do with it." He grinned at his wife. Because the only thing he needed more than his shoulder healing faster was his wife sitting astride his lap, working over the rigidness of his cock.

She pressed her lips to his with a briefness that tore a growl from Nick's throat. His hand slid over her waist, holding her close. Amelia stood from the sofa, and Nick tried to pull her back but over-stretched his sore arm in the process.

Amelia raised an eyebrow. "You must stay very still if you want my complete and unworried attention."

"Are you scolding me, wife?"

The barest hint of a wicked smile tilted up her lips. "Quite possibly. Is it working?"

She walked over to the door, shut it, and turned over the lock so they wouldn't be disturbed. Her hips swayed a little beneath her skirts as she approached him again. Nick shifted on the sofa, his cockstand straining to the point of pain against his trousers. He adjusted himself and leaned forward to shrug out of his waistcoat. The sooner they were naked, the quicker he could feel Amelia around him.

"Oh, no. Don't think I'm going to make this easy on you. We don't want to risk being caught putting your clothes back together. They stay on."

"Fine, but I want your nipples in my mouth."

Amelia's lips parted, her tongue darting out to taste them. The faintest hint of a blush painted her cheeks pink.

"But first, give me that tongue of yours. I want to suck and taste it," he said.

Leaning over him, she kissed him harder this time, yet holding back everything he wanted, teasing him. He tasted the seam of her mouth, his tongue pushing against it, but he gained no entry.

"You are terrible to tease me when I'm injured and unable to take what I want," he said.

"Shall I lecture you on the qualities of patience? I was serious when I said you had to let me do everything. You do neither of us any good if you cause further injury to yourself."

His hand cupped her breast through her dress, the feeling not nearly as satisfying with her clothes on. Her bodice tied at the back, and with one hand not working well, he knew he'd never satisfactorily secure it again.

"As I said, we will do this with our clothes on. You can't have control of every situation, Nick."

"Then give me your mouth. Let me at least taste you on my tongue."

"You say the sweetest, most provocative things to me."

But she didn't give him her mouth. No, she lifted up her skirts, placing one slippered foot on the sofa next to his thigh, opening the slit in her drawers to his rapturous gaze. His mouth watered at the slight peak of her mons and the soft down covering of her thatch.

"It can be just as alluring with our clothes on."

"Straddle my thighs." His voice had grown hoarse.

She shook her head, holding out her hand, palm up. "Give me your hand."

He did without a second's hesitation. She guided it to the soft thatch of hair covering what he wanted on his mouth. He closed his eyes and cupped her for a moment. She was slick, ready for him. His fingers slid through her folds, finding the nub of her pleasure spot. He rotated her wetness around and then shoved two fingers deep inside her.

Her fingers were tangled in his hair, holding him tight, yet keeping him afar. He pulled out of her only to slam in harder. Hooking his fingers inside her, he massaged her sheath, letting the suction hold him tight. He wanted his cock stuffing her, being milked by her. He needed to be inside her.

Opening his eyes, he pulled out of her gripping cunt and sucked the juice off his fingers. Her tongue darted out, licking her lips between the panting that had her chest rising and falling in excitement.

She brought her knee down to the sofa, half straddling him and half standing on the floor as she loosened his trousers enough to free his cock. It sprang free, hard as ever. Nick reached beneath her skirt and cupped her buttocks so he could pull her fully onto his lap. The first touch of her mons to the head of his cock nearly had him going off. He let her go to fist himself hard, to keep from coming.

That was what she did to him. Made him lose all control.

Both of her hands were tangled in his hair; she yanked his head back and leaned over him to suck on his tongue at the same moment she sank down on his cock. She stopped when his whole length stretched her. His hand rubbed at her thigh; his other lay useless over his chest. God, he wanted to throw her down on the floor and fuck them both into the ground so hard that they didn't have the strength to dress and see to the rest of their errands for the day.

Their tongues tasted each other in an open-mouthed kiss. It was a kiss that familiarized themselves with each other again. A kiss that allowed them to memorize the shape of each other's mouths, what made the other person's pleasure soar, and what passion tasted like to both of them as they made love.

"It's been too long since I've tasted you," he said. And she pulled herself up on his length only to sink back down.

"Only yesterday."

"Too long. I want to laze about in bed for weeks, take you hard, and then take you slow. I want to fuck you every imaginable way possible, learn what makes you scream loudest, what makes your cunt weep around my cock the hardest."

He sucked her tongue into his mouth, playing with it like he wanted to play with her clitoris.

"I can taste myself on you," she groaned, breathless.

"I like how you taste and want to make a feast out of that pretty little cunt of yours."

Amelia's pace quickened. Her ardor rose with each stroke of his cock inside her. He could tell by the way she pulled away from their kisses to arch her neck and stretch her body back that she was surrendering to their moment of passion. Letting go and taking everything he could give her in his limited ability to move.

"The next time we do this, we'll both be naked." He pressed a kiss against her cloth-clad and corset-covered breasts. What he would do to suck her pert nipples into his mouth right now.

"For now, we do this my way." She punctuated that statement with a slam of her pelvis against his and then rotated her hips over him, working his cock in such a way that he came before he could pull back. He shouted something incomprehensible, pumping his cock deep inside her until he was wrung out.

Nick rested his forehead against her sternum, giving himself a moment to catch his breath. She felt so damn good. Too good to be true. And yet she was his wife. She had married him and without a second thought.

Spitting on his thumb—not that he needed to make her any wetter—he pushed his hand under her skirts again and rotated the pad of his thumb around her clitoris. Her hands were in his hair, holding him tight, pulling so hard that he felt the tug at the roots. She went off like fireworks, panting and moaning around his mouth, until she couldn't breathe and had to stop moving her pelvis altogether. She jerked in his hold a few times, her sheath clasping his semi-firm cock, bringing him back to life.

She collapsed on top of him as her orgasm ebbed. His cock still flexed against the clasp of her sheath. He could stay like this all afternoon. Wouldn't that be perfect? But the next time they did this, it wouldn't be a quick coupling.

Her breathing evened out, and she pushed herself into a sitting position. When she made to pull off him, his hand squeezed her leg. "You are so beautiful when you come for me. Stay for a bit. You feel good around me. And feeling good takes away all the pain." That, and he felt a trickle of wetness slide down his bad arm. He did not want to be lectured just yet on tearing his stitches.

"You have a devil of a tongue, husband." She wiggled her bottom in his lap, his hand caressing the round globe and squeezing it. "And very wicked hands."

"All the better to make you scream, wife."

She shook her head and eventually climbed off his lap. His cock wasn't so easily sated and rested on his lap in a semi-hard position. If she sucked the head of it in her mouth, just for a second, he knew he'd be hard in an instant.

She wore a silly grin on her face, one that said she'd just spent time being intimate with her husband. He'd put that look on her face, even though he hadn't been able to do much of the pleasuring. He vowed the next time they were together he'd taste every inch of her skin.

Her gaze slipped to his arm, and her smile faltered. "Nick, you're bleeding!"

"It's nothing."

"It's *not* nothing. We need to get you upstairs so I can properly look at it."

"I pulled it. The skin is tight, and if I don't exercise it, my arm will be stiff."

"I would rather take a look at it than take your word right now. I shouldn't have listened to you at all."

With quick efficiency, she got his trousers back on but not before making his cock stand to full attention again. She pointed at him, scolding. "Not a chance. We'll resume those activities when you are better. You've only been out of bed two days, Nick. And I won't risk your having another fever because you pulled out the stitches and reopened the wound."

"I will be fine," he promised. He'd been in worse shape than this.

He grabbed her hand before she could leave him sitting on the sofa like an invalid. It was odd how his shoulder and arm were the only parts of him to be damaged when his whole body felt like it had been dragged behind a horse.

To prove that he was indeed all right, he let Amelia pull him to his feet and then followed her to the door.

Her hand fluttered against his chest as he trapped her between his body and the wall. "If you wanted to get my clothes off," he said, "you needed only to ask, and I would be more than eager to comply."

"Stop this instant. I feel terrible that you're bleeding at all."

"I don't," he said, his voice lowering. "In fact, I have no regrets."

Amelia shook her head, ignoring his insinuating tone. "Let's get you upstairs."

"If you say so." He pulled away from her and let her lead the way. He wondered how long it would be before he got them both naked and in bed.

Chapter Twelve

"We will be prepared for any scenario this time," Nick said to Amelia. And she supposed he was right, considering a note had gone to the magistrate of Highgate two days ago.

She wasn't sure she believed Nick's way of thinking, but she would rather plan for the worst than face a situation they were not prepared to meet head on. At least he'd rested for nearly a week. She hoped that was enough to keep him going while they searched for Shauley.

Traffic was slow getting out of London's core, but they were on the road to Highgate all too soon for her liking. Huxley rode outside the carriage on horseback. He insisted they couldn't go alone, not after what had happened the last time.

Nick hadn't argued with his man of affairs. Amelia was thankful for the additional help. Nick insisted he was well enough to travel and to mete out whatever revenge he thought was needed, but Amelia didn't believe it for one second. She'd wished she had been able to delay him at home longer. But Nick had grown restless the longer he remained idle.

So she'd gone along with his mad plan, and she hoped she wouldn't regret it.

"He won't be expecting you," Amelia said.

"Shauley or the vicar?"

"I imagine both."

"I don't buy into Shauley's renewed sympathy toward me, sparing me the way he did. He was buying time, distracting us both." Nick took her hand and squeezed it. "What I can't figure out is his purpose for doing so."

"I know no more than you, Nick. He let us both walk away. He had an opportunity to kill either of us. Instead, he let us live."

"Aside from saying he's gone bloody mad, I need to end that chapter in my life."

"You haven't had a nightmare since you woke from your fever," she said, her hand squeezing his ever so slightly.

Had he realized that?

"While I was in my fevered state, I felt like I cycled constantly through the past. Mostly the memory of the beating that left the scars on my back."

Amelia rested her head on his good shoulder. She knew how hard it was for him to discuss what had happened while he was at the vicarage's school. So she let him talk without prompting him.

"They wanted to break me. They wanted my surrender."

Amelia knew that was the reason he always had to be in control of a situation. Even when they made love, it was difficult for him to hand the reins to her, but he was getting better. Not that he had a lot of choice when his mobility was something of an issue. But letting her take control was also part of sharing in things equally.

"What do you want with the vicar? You've waited so long, Nick; it's hard for me to understand why you need to face him after all this time."

"For a long time I was afraid of him. Afraid of what he'd almost made me beg for. Because even though he didn't realize it, Amelia, he did break me."

She sat up and looked him in the eyes. "No one broke you, Nick. You, of all people, were made stronger by a horrible past."

He let out a short laugh and focused his gaze out the window.

Placing her hand over his cheek, she forced him to turn to look at her again. "You are the strongest, kindest, most incredible person I have ever known. Those are *not* the qualities of a man who is shattered. You rose above that past and carved out a wonderful life for yourself and for those you have taken in, including me."

"I can do all that and still have demons haunt me."

"I know all too well about personal demons, Nick. I will never forget where I came from or what happened to me. But I can't focus on that. I have to move on if I want to grow as a person. I'm not suggesting you need to grow, but you do need to forgive and move on."

"A man can only tolerate so much. What Shauley did to you was inexcusable and something I cannot ignore. We are heading back to Highgate to make things right, to make sure Shauley can never hurt another person."

"I agree that he should be stopped. But at the same time, he gave me a second chance. I don't want to waste that chance by chasing after him."

Even though that was precisely what they were doing. She had agreed to come with Nick because, despite the fact that she didn't completely agree with what he wanted to do, she would stand by him. She would always stand at his side as his partner, wife, and friend.

Amelia reminded herself for the millionth time that Huxley was close at hand and wouldn't go far from them. The magistrate for the district also promised a handful of good men on a moment's notice. They were better protected during this visit. They were ready for almost anything. Amelia looked skyward and sent up a short prayer, hoping she was right.

The one thing she had now that she hadn't had before was insight. Nick had opened up to her about his plans, and together, they'd gone over every logistical outcome and problem. Then they'd found solutions to all the possible problems that might come up. It had better be enough, because she couldn't face the prospect of nearly losing him again.

Still, she worried that he was so focused on rectifying all that had happened in the past few weeks that he was losing sight of what was really important. The school, building up this place outside of London, supporting families, and teaching children who might not otherwise have an education— those were more important than revenge, but until he saw that, she could not convince him otherwise.

While Amelia had long ago made peace with her upbringing and with the cruelty her brother had doled out, she knew every situation was different, depending on the individual. Nick would have to find that same place of peace she had. And that was something he would have to come to terms with on his own. But she would be there in any capacity he needed to find that peace. That was what you did for the person you loved.

Amelia was startled awake when they pulled to a stop. She lifted her head and looked at her husband. "I cannot believe I fell asleep."

"You've run yourself ragged taking care of me."

She wiped her eyes and looked out the window. They'd arrived at the same inn where they'd roomed prior to the last incident with Shauley.

The proprietor and his wife stood outside in the courtyard, waiting to greet them. As Nick took her hand so she could step down from the carriage, the innkeeper's wife said, "We have prepared our best room for you."

"It's appreciated," Nick said shortly, making Amelia cringe at the coldness of his voice. It was easy to forget how he treated everyone outside the trusted individuals he cared for.

Amelia approached the woman and took her hands between her own. "I'm happy you would have us again."

"We all want to stop this madman. He's threatening our very livelihoods. He needs to be captured," the proprietor said.

"I take it you are assisting the magistrate?" Nick asked.

The innkeeper nodded at Nick's query.

Nick nodded sharply before he took Amelia's arm to lead her inside.

We are here, she wanted to say. *Now what?* Did they wait? Did they leave right away for the cabin? Anxiety built inside her. Making her hate this whole situation with renewed disgust.

Nick turned to her when they were in their room. "Dinner?"

"You're going to casually ask if I want dinner?"

"I am. Then I'm going to feed it to you," he said with a hint of wickedness and suggestion in his comment.

"We came here with a task in mind. Are you trying to distract me?"

"That's very possible. You are tense, and we need to approach this with a clear mind."

"I find it difficult to wait here casually when so many things can go wrong tomorrow."

"I plan on visiting Brother John today," he said, which was news to her. "We didn't come here to spend our time in leisure, but I do want some time alone with you before I leave."

Amelia took off her bonnet and set it on the writing table by the window. She looked down at the courtyard. Huxley leaned against the wall at the front gate, hat tipped low over his brow, while he smoked a cigar. He would act as the first point of contact. As a guard to her if she left the inn.

"We already agreed I would attend the cabin with you. You cannot change the plan now that we are here."

"That doesn't mean I won't try to convince you to stay behind. The thought of any danger coming to you pains me."

"Brother John is no threat to me."

"But Shauley is. And it is possible he is staying somewhere near that cabin. If he shows up again, he'll likely be less forgiving, and if he wants to hurt me, he'll go after you."

"One worry at a time, love. We can't assume the worst. Not yet. Because it's like we are living in fear, allowing that man to rule our every action."

Nick walked toward her—more like prowled and ready to pounce.

Amelia backed up. The back of her legs hit the desk, stalling any further escape.

"You have that look in your eyes," she said, breathless from a mere glance. She wanted to pinch herself for being so easily distracted.

"What look is that?"

"The one telling me you want me in bed."

He grinned and cocked an eyebrow. "It will prove to be a great distraction. It'll take our minds off the more pressing issues occupying our thoughts."

He came closer. She had nowhere to go, so she put her hand out to stall him, but all that did was draw him harder into her touch. She spread her hand over the firmness of his chest; her palm rested over his heartbeat.

"As long as you don't use this as a distraction to leave me behind. I'll never forgive you if you do."

Nick pulled one of her gloves off and let it fall between them. "I wouldn't think of it," he said before sealing his mouth over hers.

True to his word, Amelia accompanied Nick to the cabin, though he did grumble about it for a while, hoping she would change her mind. When he realized her mind was made, he gave in to her request, and Huxley argued that she should stay behind until she firmly told him it wasn't his choice.

His wife, a woman of her own mind, would not be deterred.

They'd taken their usual mounts from the stable hand, saddled, and rode off just after they'd had an early dinner. Huxley followed unobtrusively behind them as they rode deeper into the forest.

"Are you nervous?" Amelia asked him.

"No." He was so close to finally facing his nightmares that he could taste it. And it tasted like victory.

Amelia was right; while revenge had been the only thing on his mind since the Murray lands had come up for sale, there was more happening here than that. He wasn't an optimistic person, but Amelia made him want to adopt the positive outlook she had on everything.

His leg bumped into hers every now and again, reminding him that there were more important things than revenge. Like Amelia. Her love. Her beauty that shone so bright on the outside it dulled the image of every other women he'd ever known. It also dulled the ugliness that had always been a part of his life.

"Have I told you how much I love you?" he asked.

She gave him a shy smile and looked at him through lowered lashes.

"You can never say it too often. I love you more than I can ever put in words, which means I'll just have to show you all the ways I love you every day," she responded.

He stood in his stirrups and leaned toward her to kiss her on the lips. "If we were out riding for our own purpose, I'd haul you off that horse right now and take you on the ground."

Her face flamed. "You can't say such things. Huxley is close behind."

"That's the other reason I won't do exactly that."

"Nick." She pointed toward a grouping of trees.

"You, there! Halt!" Nick sat hard in his saddle and shouted after Brother John. He dug his heels into his mount, speeding up his horse, so the old man didn't try his disappearing act again.

He could hear the hooves of Amelia's horse not far behind him.

"Mr. Riley." John set his basket down on a tree stump raised out of the ground. "Ah, Mrs. Riley. It's a pleasure to have your company again."

"I'm not buying your act of contrition, old man," Nick said before Amelia could respond.

"I'm not sure what you mean."

"I asked you before, but you didn't answer honestly. Do you remember me?"

Brother John looked at Amelia.

"She's not going anywhere, monk. What you have to say can be said in her presence."

A look of sadness washed over the old man's expression. "I remember them all, don't I?"

"Who are *them all?*" Nick asked.

"The boys. All of you." His gaze glazed over and grew unfocused.

"Why do you still live here?"

John suddenly became attentive as he contemplated his answer. "The vicar's the last one."

"The last what?" Nick asked, confused.

"The last of the old parish. The last of those who used God's name for evil."

That was not the answer Nick had expected. "Where is he?"

"The vicar?"

Nick nodded; Amelia stayed silent at his side. "And Shauley," he said.

"Shauley? You mean Michael? I haven't seen him for some time. He used to sit with the vicar for hours at a time."

"For what purpose?" Nick swung his leg over the horse and jumped off the animal. He wanted to be on even ground as he looked Brother John in the eye.

Brother John lifted his basket. "Walk an old man home, Mr. Riley. I think we have a lot to discuss."

Nick held his horse's reins up to Amelia, which she took without comment.

"I'll humor you, but you better have the answers I need. I won't play your games. Not another goddamn day of games from you and your followers." Nick arched his arm in the direction from which he and Amelia had come. "I have men in the wood, ready to step in if something untoward should come about."

"I will cause you and your wife no harm, Mr. Riley. On that you have my word."

"Your word isn't worth anything, Brother John. We both know what kind of man you are, what you participated in."

"Do we?"

For the first time in years, that small comment had the ability to make Nick question himself and his motives. He shook the feeling off.

The old man picked up his basket and walked on, not waiting for Nick; he must have assumed Nick wasn't far behind. They made it to the cabin in less than ten minutes. Amelia dismounted and let the horses graze.

"There's a table around the back. Chairs too. Come, sit with me a while." John approached Nick, coming close to whisper something. It took everything in Nick to stand still, to not recoil from the vileness this man represented in Nick's nightmares. "You may not want your wife to hear what I have to say."

"I will make that call if I have to; it's not your decision to make."

"As you wish."

At the rustic wooden table, John pulled out the contents from his basket and picked through the berries, choosing which were good and bad. The bad he tossed toward his vegetable patch.

"Why didn't you stop them that day they beat me?"

"Some wounds never heal, do they?" John's blue gaze, while cloudy, seemed startlingly clear for his age. And in the old man, Nick saw something of himself.

That couldn't be right.

"I will not play guessing games with you."

The monk held out his hand, motioning to the chair folded and leaning against the table. Nick opened it and settled himself into the seat.

"I was the same age you were when I first attended the vicarage school."

"Do you want my sympathy?"

"We wear the same scars, Mr. Riley."

"Do we? To which scars do you refer? Because I carry more than one kind."

"We all do. But I'm referring to the ones across your back."

Nick tensed.

"I see disbelief in your expression. Mrs. Riley," John said in a louder voice, drawing Amelia's attention, "would you mind walking around the front of the house for a few minutes? I have something of a personal nature to show your husband."

She hesitated.

"Give us three minutes," Nick said, and after she nodded her agreement and turned around as asked, he continued. "What is it you have to show me, Brother John?"

As nimble as a man much younger than the age he wore on his face, John pulled his habit straight over his head and turned around. Nick's jaw cracked, but he made no other sound to give away what he was feeling. Hell, he didn't know what he felt, other than a strange kinship that seemed wrong.

The scars on John's back were similar to his own. But that did not make their hardships the same.

"You can cover yourself," Nick said, looking away from the sight that was so familiar to him. John pulled his habit back on and tied the rope around his waist. "If you were a student like me, why did you allow the others to degrade the boys? To act the way they did without taking action against it?"

"I tried. On more than one occasion. It was no use. Their treatment escalated into something far more depraved. So instead, I focused on dividing the rectory, destroying it from within. It took years, but I accomplished it with the help of the other student with whom you attended."

Shauley. That was the last thing Nick expected to hear, and he was sure his face showed that astonishment. "If Shauley is the good guy, why is he hiding in the background, doing all sorts of misdeeds to get his point across and to achieve his revenge in whatever form it is he seeks?"

"I can only tell you what I know of his character from the school."

"What does he speak of with the vicar?"

"That I do not know. Their conversations are private, and it is not my place to pry."

"Can you tell me why you live here with the vicar?"

"I have taken away all his luxuries. Removed him from the comforts of the life to which he'd grown accustomed. I have forced him to live by the hand of God. It should be no burden to a man of his faith, but every day he struggles. Every day he atones in self-hatred."

"None of this excuses you from the fact that you failed to protect the young men who entered that school. You should have tried harder."

"It does not. But I have prayed every day that they have all found their way in life, that they have pulled themselves up and made something important of their lives."

"I want to see the vicar."

"Of course."

Brother John led him around the house and opened the door to the cabin. It was dark and musty inside. Nick looked at Amelia. She came toward him and took his hand in hers.

"Do you want me to go inside with you?" she asked.

"I need to do this myself."

"I'll be out here with Huxley." Huxley leaned against the fence that surrounded the vegetable patch. Close enough to assist, far enough to give them privacy.

Nick kissed his wife on the mouth and left her in the front of the cabin.

Chapter Thirteen

Faced with the devil himself, Nick found he was at a loss for words. The man he had built up into a grand monster and whom he feared most of his life had been reduced to a husk of a human being over the years.

Looking at the old man in front of him, Nick saw what happened to a man who was full of bitterness.

Nick turned and looked at Brother John. "Can he hear me?"

"I can hear just fine," the vicar said distastefully and rather obnoxiously. So his hearing wasn't perfect, but he could make out Nick's words well enough. "What is it you want?"

Brother John nodded and motioned for Nick to continue. Nick turned to stare in shock at the aged man before him. He was no longer the monster Nick had built him up to be, only a man broken by the life he led, by the hatred that made his soul as black as tar.

The vicar coughed, the sound like that of a dog with a broken voice. From his lap, he lifted a ragged handkerchief to cover his mouth. The yellow, threadbare linen came away bloody.

"Get on with it," he said when his coughing fit subsided. "It's too late in the day for visitors. I need to rest." He made a shooing motion with his hands. Nick stood firmly planted to the dirt floor.

Nick studied the interior with new eyes. Indeed, this was back to God, living from what the land provided. No amenities, no luxuries that new houses provided. The bare necessities of life were all that existed here.

"I've hated you most of my life," Nick said, stepping farther into the room.

The vicar turned his head up and glared at him. The man that had frightened Nick as a boy still lurked in that cloudy gaze.

"Who in hell are you?" he said, coughing again.

Nick shook his head, more for himself than for the benefit of the vicar. "I want to say I'm too late, but really, I'm just glad to see you reduced to this half life and pitiful existence."

"Do I know you? Where's Michael? Michael!" the vicar shouted.

"He's not here to help you. And when I do get my hands on him, he'll be hanged. I once thought it would give me great pleasure to turn you over to the authorities, to have you arrested for sodomy. For the indecencies and your depravity. But now…now I want you to live out your life. Or what's left of it. It looks to be a painful end for you, old man."

The vicar grunted. Nick looked around the small cabin again, saying good-bye to his hatred, his need for retribution. None of it mattered anymore in the face of death. He shook his head and laughed quietly to himself before turning his back on his past and stepping out into the light, where Amelia waited for him, twisting her gloved hands together.

She didn't say anything and a look of puzzlement robbed her expression when she saw his smile. "Is everything all right?" she asked.

"Yes." He pulled Amelia into his arms and held on to her for dear life, squeezing the breath out of her as he did so.

"Nick, what is this?"

"This is the close of one chapter in my old life and the opening of a new one into ours."

Amelia pressed her elbows into his chest and leaned back to look at him. "The vicar?"

"Is nothing and no one to hold sway over me for a moment longer. He is someone I created to be larger than life. A boy's nightmare that grew into something alive. I realize now that while my hate was fruitless, it made me into the man I am. Had I not become this person you see before you, our paths might never have crossed."

"Oh, Nick." Amelia's eyes filled with tears. "What about the things he did to you and the other boys?"

"We forgive, and we move on. Is that what you told me? If we don't"—he motioned to the tiny clearing around the cabin—"we become this. The vicar is short for this life, and when he goes, I like to believe Lucifer himself will collect the vicar's soul for eternal damnation."

Nick rubbed his thumb along her cheek, catching the first fall of tears. All the hate and need for revenge was gone. Miraculously gone. The only thing he felt right now was his love for her. And that truly was all that mattered.

The pounding of horses' hooves reached their ears long before anyone could see who rode toward them.

Nick set Amelia behind him; Huxley lifted the back of his jacket and pulled out a pistol he had hidden there. Nick was too far from his saddlebags to pull out his weapon, but he reached into his boot and pulled out a steel folding knife he had carried when he was popular in the fighting rings. The thugs that would come after him…they were no match against his brute strength and his precise aim; the same went for the rider coming in on them fast.

At this point, his presence should have been no surprise.

Shauley.

"Shit," Nick muttered under his breath. Nick didn't think it was a coincidence that Shauley happened to show up on the day Nick arrived in Highgate. He turned to Brother John. "How did you send word to him we were here?"

"I have no way of contacting Mr. Shauley. He likely followed you from London."

Nick couldn't fault the monk on what might very well be the truth. Damn it. Shauley had been at their backs this whole time.

Huxley spit on the ground and shrugged his shoulders. The man was a born and bred fighter and the chance of Shauley's putting one over on either Huxley or Nick was unlikely. The shot to Nick's shoulder was a fluke and because Nick had least expected that kind of reaction from Shauley.

This time, he was prepared for anything.

Shauley's horse skidded to a stop, legs dancing as it kicked up dust.

"I always knew you could never trust the word of a woman," Shauley said. "A shame you didn't listen, Mrs. Riley."

Amelia didn't respond, for which Nick was thankful. The less either of them said to set off Shauley the better they would all fare. While Nick was armed and ready to fight, Shauley had come prepared with his pistol again.

"I should have aimed better, Nick. You're up and about far too soon for the injury I caused you."

"Why did you want to keep me from here?"

"Can't you guess?"

"The vicar is an old man. What purpose do you have for seeing to his needs, for visiting him at all?"

"He is the only person who sees me exactly as I am."

"And what of your employer?"

"A means to keep connected to this part of the country. You took that away from me. You took everything away from me."

"Is that what the vicar had you believe? That you and he were alike? While I agree you both strongly resemble monsters better suited for hell, you are not alike unless you committed the same crimes as he."

Shauley made a face that said he abhorred the type of behavior in which the vicar participated.

Brother John had somehow convinced Shauley of that. Had seized upon that opportunity to set up the cabin and keep the vicar away from the village and other boys to whom he could cause injury. Now, it didn't seem like the vicar could do much damage to anyone except to himself. Everything was clear now, but none of it negated the fact that Shauley had to pay for his crimes and answer to the murder of Amelia's brother.

Nick felt nothing but pity for Shauley. Shauley had been easy prey to an older man's constant abuse. And the worst of it was that Shauley—sick, twisted, and depraved Shauley—was the victim here. A victim molded by evil for so long that he had become evil.

Brother John stepped forward. "Mr. Shauley—"

The report of the pistol sent Nick flying into action before he even realized he'd thrown Amelia to the ground, covering her with his body. A second shot followed the first as Brother John fell to his knees, a bloom of red filling his forehead as his gaze dimmed and grew vacant.

Shauley was reloading his pistol, and Nick knew he couldn't give the man another chance to aim that weapon.

Nick charged toward the horse and its rider without a second thought. Nick's fist flew into Shauley's face; the resounding crack of his jaw and the spray of blood that followed only fueled Nick's newfound rage. He continued to pummel Shauley's face, taking him right off the horse and to the dirt.

"Your reign of terror is over." Nick spit out the blood that had filled his own mouth. He must have knocked a tooth loose on his way back down to the ground.

Huxley's boots came into view, reminding Nick he wasn't alone. With his knee pressed into Shauley's chest, Nick held him down.

His fist lowered, Nick surveyed the area around them. Amelia was where he'd thrown her onto the ground, tears washing down her face, eyes red and raw. The crook of her arm muffled her sobs where she held it over her face, but he read the relief in her eyes when their gazes clashed and stuck.

They had a moment of thanks that they were both safe.

Huxley held out a length of rope, which Nick took before roughly turning Shauley over and tying his hands behind his back. Huxley grabbed Shauley's legs and bound them together.

"I'll tie him to the horse," Huxley said, as if this were something they did with regularity.

"I'll see to my wife," Nick said, without taking his eyes off his wife.

She was heaving in great gulps of air when he approached. She didn't look up at him; she stared at the spot where Brother John had fallen face forward onto the ground. Nick didn't need to check the old man; he was dead with a shot between the eyes.

Kneeling next to her, Nick pulled her into his arms and rubbed his hand over her hair. "Shh," he said. "I have you now. We're going to be all right. We have made it this far. We can make it through anything."

By the time Amelia and Nick arrived back at the inn, it was dark. He took her immediately up to their room. All Amelia could think was that an innocent man had died, and she had been helpless to stop it.

Nick hadn't left her side once Huxley tied up Shauley on his horse and headed back to the inn ahead of them. Nick was a constant she needed if she was going to make it through this ordeal with her sanity intact.

And Shauley—right now, he was on his way back to London to be tried for his crimes. Huxley had accompanied the magistrate to ensure a smooth ride without hiccups along the way.

She could hardly believe it was over. They'd been working toward this point, and in the blink of an eye, it was just over.

Shauley would not be given a reprieve; he would hang, and Amelia knew that as sure as the sun rose each day. Shauley had confessed to his involvement in her brother's death, allowing for closure on both her and Nick's pasts. How odd that it came from the same source, when prior to Amelia's coming to London, she and Nick had been worlds apart.

"Why are you sitting here in the dark?"

Amelia looked toward the door. Light filtered in behind Nick. She must have been sitting in bed for some time. She hadn't the energy to get up. Hadn't the energy to even shed another tear.

"I was lost in my thoughts," she responded.

"Care to share them?"

She looked away from him. "I can barely make sense of them."

"Try."

"Brother John didn't deserve what fate delivered him today."

This caused Nick to frown. "No more than your brother deserved to die, I suppose."

"Does it make me an awful person to be glad Brother John is dead and that you're safe? That Shauley chose to shoot him before hurting you?"

Tears trickled out of the corner of her eyes again. Guilt was eating her up. Guilt that someone had died in place of Nick being hurt again.

Nick leaned over the table and lit a few candles, just enough for them to see by.

"It doesn't make you a bad person, Amelia. It makes you human."

"I could have lost you." Her lips trembled.

"You didn't." Nick kissed her forehead and urged her to stand. He helped her toward the washbasin. "Let me wash the dirt from your hands, Amelia. Let's wash the day away. We likely won't ever forget it, but together, we can move on."

Amelia stared down at her palms. Her hands had been tightly clasped in her lap for so long that she'd forgotten they were scraped nearly raw. Scratches dotted with bits of blood left streaks of red all over her.

Before she could protest what Nick was doing, he sunk both her hands in the washbasin. She hissed in a breath.

"I'm sorry. They need to be cleaned; then we'll check the rest of you for injuries."

"I have none. Nick, I just want to climb into bed and lie with you. I can't face anyone right now. I don't even want to talk. I just want to close my eyes and be thankful we still have each other. I want your arms around me, keeping me safe."

Wrapping a linen around her hands, he dried her carefully, patting the water away. He removed her outer clothes, letting them fall on the floor. He didn't remove her chemise or corset. There was nothing sexual about the way he handled her. He tucked her into bed, stripped out of his own clothes, and lay behind her, holding her in his arms, her back pressed to his chest. Neither said a word as they gently touched and caressed each other for what might have been hours.

"Nick?" Amelia whispered.

"Hmmm," he mumbled sleepily.

"I love you."

Nick moved the hair away from her neck, tucking it behind her ear, and kissed the soft curve of her neck. "You are my life, Amelia. Without you, I am nothing."

And she was nothing without him. Today, as tragic and awful as it was, had put them on the path to their future. After today, they could face any obstacle and become stronger together. But the key to that was always in trusting in each other, being honest, and respecting each other's boundaries.

Amelia fell asleep with that thought on her mind.

CHAPTER FOURTEEN

Two weeks later...

Amelia looked down at the frills on the white- and blue-silk dress that left little to the imagination for her upper half, completely baring her shoulders and high décolletage. The width of the sleeves where it wrapped around the middle of her arm couldn't be more than two finger-widths. The bustle gathered at her derrière had shots of burgundy silk woven through it, adding just a hint of color to the ensemble. The material was so fine and delicate she was afraid to wear it outside the house.

"You are a sight to behold," Nick said as he walked into their bedchamber from his dressing room.

She got the shock of her life when she faced him. "You shaved your beard!"

"I needed a change." He self-consciously rubbed his hand over his cheek and jaw.

"I will have to beat off the other women."

He looked sharp in his evening tails. His eyes were piercing as he leveled them on her with a mix of hunger and appreciation.

Nick smiled, and she nearly melted into the floor. He had dimples that would make every woman who saw them faint dead away.

She walked toward him and kissed him, lingering and getting a sense of how different it felt with the scruff of his beard gone. "Won't you tell me where we are going?"

"I did; we are having dinner with Hart and a few friends."

"I feel overdressed."

"You're not. This dress suits you and is perfect for the occasion."

Her eyes widened. "So you *are* keeping something from me. Tell me what the occasion is, please."

He pressed his mouth to hers in a brief kiss. "You'll find out soon enough. Now, turn around."

Nick wrapped a cord around her neck. Amelia touched the soft velvet as Nick tied it in a bow at her nape and let the ends dangle down between her shoulder blades. He kissed the side of her neck, his breath hot on her pulse that sped up every second she remained in his embrace.

"We will never leave the house if you continue doing that," she said, turning and letting her arms rest over his shoulders.

He lowered her wrist, kissing the delicate inside before swiping his tongue around the pulse that drummed in time with her heart. Amelia's lips parted on a sigh. Nick moved abruptly back and tied a band of burgundy velvet around one wrist and then the other.

"There is no other word for you but stunning," he said, admiring her at arm's length. He handed her gloves to her. "We'd better leave before we find ourselves decidedly underdressed and naked under the bedcovers."

She bit her cheek to keep from grinning, but it was useless. Nick's good humor was intoxicating and consuming.

"Perhaps that's where I prefer to be." She hated large functions. With a burning passion, she hated them. But she would do what Nick wanted, as they had done very few functions since their marriage had been announced.

"Just wait until I get you in the carriage. You won't be grinning; you'll be moaning my name."

"Is that a promise?"

His only answer was a wink before he took her hand and walked down the stairs with her.

Their carriage pulled up in front of the Langtry, which was Hart's hotel. When they didn't head in the direction of the dining room, Amelia pulled Nick to a stop. "Nick, I know we planned this function, but I'm still nervous. We have seen so few of your friends and some not at all since we married. Tell me what to expect at the very least."

Nick kissed both her cheeks and her then her lips. "I cannot give away the surprise. But I promise it's one you'll relish."

They walked arm in arm up to the second level and entered a long hallway Amelia had never been down before. There were half a dozen doors, all painted in gold leaf; by all appearances, they were separate rooms in the hotel.

They approached a set of double doors at the end of the hall, and Amelia felt her heart rate increase, and her palms grew sweaty beneath her lace gloves.

"You look gorgeous, love. And whatever tonight brings, just know that you are my world. And I want to shower you in everything that is precious and perfect."

"You're not helping matters any," she said, her voice pitched higher than normal. She wasn't sure she was cut out for surprises.

Nick rapped on the doors, and they opened simultaneously to reveal…

A small ensemble that played Strauss for no one. The room was small, and it looked like it served as a private dining hall when needed. The floor was a patterned hardwood that was heavily polished and gleamed under the crystal chandelier that hung above their heads. Windows flanked one wall in the room and were covered in golden velvet curtains.

One of the serving staff came over with a tray of champagne flutes.

"I thought we were meeting Hart and, I assumed, Lord and Lady Burley."

"After our first dance, they'll join us."

"Why are we here?"

Nick leaned in close to her ear and softly said, "Because I wanted you to have your very own ball."

"But there are no guests."

"Would you have preferred I invited half of London?"

She shook her head. "How well you know me."

Nick held his arm out for her to take, which she did. He walked them forward. The ensemble of instruments took their cue from him.

"Nick. Thank you for arranging this…" Amelia's voice came out wistful. It was turning into a magical night.

"I had help," was his response as he turned her about and bowed before her. "I believe the first dance is mine," he said.

She laughed, because he was the only person here with whom to dance. "It's a good thing I don't have eyes for any other man."

The music ensemble started a familiar tune that was lively and quick.

It was the first song they'd ever danced to. The first time the boundaries between secretary and employer were irrevocably severed, and they became so much more; the beginning of what they were now.

This was the song they'd danced to all those weeks ago in the absinthe café. A mazurka, she thought it was called. The steps were fast, the pace invigorating. She inhaled deeply as her husband took her hand and brought her closer to his body.

"I believe you already know the steps to this particular piece."

She smiled up at him. "I believe I do."

The fast steps were exactly as she remembered as they trotted around the ballroom, laughing and holding each other. Making a ruckus for only two people. But she didn't care.

What Nick had done for her here…

It was beyond all her imaginings.

Amelia threw her arms around her husband's shoulders as the song wound down to a finale. She wished they could lock themselves in this moment and not share it with anyone. And they could, in a way, but she had a feeling this couldn't last all night, and not because she didn't want it to but because she didn't think her feet would stand for it.

Nick grabbed her up, lifting her clear off her feet, and swung her around in a circle, her dress fanning out around them.

Amelia arched back and let go of his shoulders, letting him hold her up, spinning her about. And she let herself be free for a single moment and laughed at the joy she felt bursting out from her heart.

She didn't care what kind of spectacle they made to the ensemble. What mattered was that their love could not be faked, could not be denied. They had found that place where they were both happy. And maybe that had been Nick's intention in throwing this surprise for her. Maybe it hadn't been. But in this moment, everything in her life was perfect, and it could never have been this way without Nick in her life.

The revelation and realization was glorious and beautiful.

"Thank you," she said when he set her down. She stood in the middle of the room, looking at him through lowered lashes.

"We missed celebrating our wedding. I won't take the small things for granted. The things we can control in our lives we will enjoy to the fullest."

She felt herself blush from the tips of her toes all the way up to the roots of her hair.

He kissed her hands and whispered, "I love you more than life itself, Amelia."

"You are the most wonderful husband in the world, Nicholas Riley, and I am honored to be your wife."

"And you are the most beautiful bride I could ask for."

She threw her arms around him. "I love you, Nick. Always and forever."

He returned the embrace and moved them easily into another dance, something slower, a song that allowed them to look into each other's eyes. "And I love you more than words alone can offer. I will endeavor to show you all the ways I love you as we grow old together, Amelia Riley."

Highgate, London, 1883

Amelia took Nick's hand and carefully stepped down from the barouche. It was warm for September, and the heat fatigued her so quickly. Nick kissed her forehead, and rested his hand against her ever-growing belly.

"How do you feel?" he asked.

"Tired. But I'm excited to see the work that has been done on Caldon Manor."

Sera hopped down next to Amelia. "It's marvelous, Nick," his sister said. "It amazes me the amount of work that can be accomplished in the course of a year."

Amelia shielded her eyes against the sun and stared up at the house. Scaffolding still surrounded the building, but it would be coming down in a month's time.

The foreman approached them. "Mr. Riley," he said.

"Douglass." Nick shook his hand. "The progress is astounding."

"We still have a lot to do on the interior, but she's coming along nicely."

"I have a painter standing at the ready the moment you are ready."

"There's some structural work to be done on the upper floors, relaying of the under-floor and fixing the plaster that's deteriorated with time."

"Can we look inside?" Sera asked both men.

The foreman wrung his hands around his hat and glanced quietly toward Amelia's distended stomach.

"It's not a bother, Douglass," Amelia said to ease his discomfort with the situation. "I need to walk some anyway. Being cramped up in a carriage that long makes for baby somersaults all evening."

Amelia kissed her husband's smooth cheek and threaded her arm through Olive's. Olive used to be the kitchen maid but was training to be a lady's maid. She'd been in Nick's employ since she was no more than a frightened child, afraid to even speak. With the loving care of Nick's household, she'd eventually found her voice and had become a valued member of their home. Olive also made a wonderful companion and had been helpful during Amelia's pregnancy, which had started with too many days of sickness to count. Thank goodness the illness had been short lived, lasting only a month.

"We won't be long," Nick promised, his sister walking toward the house already. He seemed reluctant to leave her. He was afraid she would have the baby any day now and miss the event. She had at least another month to go, but she liked that Nick cared so much.

Amelia and Olive followed a path toward the trees in search of some shade, which they found at the edge of the wood. The old wooden fence that lined the property had been replaced with a stone wall, a boundary for the school yard. They sat on the wall now, as it was only two and a half feet tall.

"Can I get you refreshment, Mrs. Riley?" Olive asked.

Amelia shook her head, her hand absently rubbing over her stomach, easing the tightening, something her doctor had called Braxton Hicks, which happened frequently when she was on her feet walking too long. Not that they had come very far to sit on the wall. "I don't need anything just yet. If I take refreshment we will have to make more stops than I'm willing to on the way home."

Amelia used her fan on her face, trying to cool the heat that had infused her while sitting in the sun most of the carriage ride to Highgate.

"Do you suppose they'll be done with the house for summer?" Olive asked.

"I hope so. Sera has her heart set on it. I know some of the families whose children will attend will be moving to Highgate after the winter season."

"Nick has a way of getting what he wants," Olive observed. She always called Nick by his Christian name and Amelia assumed it was because he was like a father figure to her, having saved Olive from a terrible fate. Nick never corrected the young woman, so Amelia didn't either.

"There my husband comes now," Amelia said with an amused expression and a shake of her head. He was constantly worried for her welfare and terrified he would miss the birth of their child.

"I wanted to see how you fared," he said.

Olive moved away, giving them privacy when Nick sat beside her on the wall.

"You needn't worry so much for me, Nick. I am well enough to sit here for a spell before we head over to the inn."

"The ground isn't even here, if you should fall…"

"I'm not likely to break, and we both know Olive can take care of my needs when you aren't around."

Nick wrapped his arm around her shoulder, pulling her into his side. His other hand curved over her belly, rubbing it possessively. He couldn't seem to refrain from touching the distended bump, even when they were in public.

She didn't mind the attention when they were alone, but when they were in public, they tended to garner a lot of uncomfortable looks from people around them.

"There are thirty workers milling around outside today," she said, blushing.

Nick's gaze was steady on hers, his hand not moving away from her stomach. "Then let them see how much you mean to me."

Amelia rested her hand over her husbands. "Will this one attend the school here?"

"Eventually. I would want nothing more than for our children to be taught by my sister."

Amelia smiled. She felt the same way. Sera was such a wonderful friend, and sister-in-law. "This baby will be surrounded by so much love."

"As my sister and I were growing up."

Tears filled Amelia's eyes. She wiped them away. "I don't know why I'm so sensitive," she said in apology. She knew her husband hated to see her cry.

He kissed her carefully on the lips, his hand at her back now, holding her close.

Amelia held onto his arm and her hat, which had come loose the closer he got.

"Nick, what are you doing?"

Nick knew how she felt about being the focal point in a crowd, but he seemed less and less able to keep his hands off her the fatter she'd grown with child.

"I can't wait to get you alone back at the inn."

She swallowed back the nervousness that built in her throat. "You can't say such things."

"No one can hear us." He kissed her again, their lips lingering longer this time. "And I know how insatiable you've grown these past months."

She was constantly desperate for his touch. She thought with a growing belly she would want to spend less time in their bedroom, but the opposite seemed to be true.

"Let's leave Olive here with my sister. They can eat lunch from the basket we prepared, and enjoy an afternoon out here until the carriage comes back," he said, already standing and assisting her to her feet.

"Absolutely not."

Nick looked around them before focusing on the path that led to the wood. "Walk with me."

She raised her eyebrow. "I don't think I'm in any shape for a scandalous interlude in the middle of Highgate forest."

"Humor me," he said pulling her along. She went, because she knew how her husband was when his mind was set on something. He asked Olive to wait for them at the carriage, giving them more privacy as he took the worn path away from Caldon Manor.

They took their time, letting her walk slowly so she didn't trip over any upturned roots or exposed rocks.

When they were alone, he turned her to face him. His hands caressed her cheeks, then rubbed along her arms.

"Why were you desperate to get me alone?"

"To do this." He lowered his mouth again, knocking her hat back, which dislodged her hatpin and had the hat falling to the ground. She ignored it, because her hands were wrapped around her husband's shoulders, keeping him close.

His lips separated hers before his tongue gently slipped into her mouth. His hand moved over the side of her belly, rotating. She knew if they were in their bedchambers right now, their clothes would start coming off. But they couldn't be so carefree out here in the middle of the wood.

When they pulled apart, she asked, "What has gotten into you?"

"Watching you glow on the carriage ride here, I wanted nothing more than to ravage your mouth then."

Amelia looked away. "Whatever will I do with you, my wicked husband?"

"Indulge me," he said as he stole her breath away in a kiss that left her panting when he pulled away again.

"We should head back to the inn now."

"I knew you'd see it my way once I got you alone."

"You are forever getting me alone. I'm amazed we manage to get dressed and out of our room most days."

She took his hand and made it only a step away from him before he pulled her back against his chest, both of his hands molding to her stomach.

"In a minute," he said, his voice hoarse, and his desire pressing into her lower back.

"Nick." Her voice was hoarse and filled with need. Her head leaned back against his shoulder and he kissed her neck. Her breasts felt heavy and sensitive, her core was slick, aching.

"I want to take you here."

The breath left her in a rush. She couldn't say no—instead, she nodded.

Nick lifted her clear off her feet and walked over to a fallen tree. He set her down and had her press her hands against the wood, which was as high as her hips. He lifted her skirts in the back and pulled and worked the buttons free on his trousers with a curse. He sunk into her before she took her next breath. Her nails dug into the bark as she spread her legs farther apart for him to sink deeper into her. He was slow as he pumped in and out of her, careful of her stomach, careful to hold her up as he fucked her from behind.

All he had to do was touch her and she was close to orgasm. "Nick."

"Don't wait, I want you coming around my cock."

His words set her off, and she felt her whole body tighten before it released in perfect bliss. She shouted, quieting the birds that chirped around them.

She couldn't hold her weight on her arms anymore and started to fall against the tree. Nick grabbed onto her and sat on the forest floor, her astride his thighs. She was too out of breath to move, which was all right, because Nick thrust shallowly into her, one hand squeezing her breast through her dress before he emptied himself in her and stilled.

Neither of them moved, they were both out of breath. "My knees are starting to hurt," she said.

Nick lifted them both off the ground, fixing the back of her skirts before putting his clothes back in order.

Amelia was flushed and hotter than ever. She took a handkerchief out to wipe away the sweat on her brow. Would everyone know what they had been up to? Embarrassment washed through her.

"You look beautiful," Nick said, kissing her forehead.

"I cannot believe we just did that."

Amelia searched the ground for her hat, and found it twenty feet away. Nick retrieved it before she could bend over and collect it herself. He dusted it off before leaning over and picking up her hatpin.

"We need to get back to your sister," she said.

"We need to get back to our inn room." He turned her to face him.

She smiled. She did want to be alone with him again. She couldn't understand how she could want to be intimate when she had a growing belly that kept them from easily embracing. And while she felt uncomfortable most of the time, when they were together, all that mattered was the two of them.

"Then let's get back to the privacy of our rented rooms."

He gave her a cocky smile. "You are more beautiful than ever," he said again.

"You're just filling my head with platitudes so I'm not embarrassed when we return to the carriage."

"No one will believe we did anything but walk through the wood."

She went on her tiptoes and kissed him lightly on the lips. "Thank you. I think that was precisely what I needed after spending the past two hours in a carriage."

"I would do anything for you, Amelia."

"I know, and that is part of the reason I love you so much."

"And I love you." His hand lowered to her stomach again. He seemed as helpless to keep his hands off it as she was. He leaned over and kissed the bump before taking her hand and leading her back to the house.

She knew she grinned like a fool the whole way back. And she was sure their slightly rumpled state was obvious, but they didn't get one side-glance as Nick eventually handed her up into the carriage and sat beside her, his arm around her shoulders as he whispered in her ear. "I want to make you blush for the rest of the day."

She hid her head in his shoulder. "Your sister is across from us."

"And she knows how much in love we are." He placed his hand on her chin and turned her head up to his. "I have never known the kind of love I have for you. You make me whole. You alone make me a better man."

And because his words made her teary-eyed, she kissed him full on the mouth in front of her lady's maid and his sister just as the horses pulled forward. Love knew no bounds, for her shyness had melted with those words.

Witness Amelia and Nicholas's love story from the very beginning with

DESIRE ME NOW

and

DESIRE ME MORE

Available now from Avon Impulse.

DESIRE ME NOW

He charged out of the darkness to her rescue…

Amelia Grant has just escaped her lecherous employer
with nothing but the clothes on her back.
In the predawn hours of London, a horse and carriage
comes barreling down on her, and a stranger rushes to her
aid, sweeping her off her feet…

There was something dark and dangerous about
Nicholas Riley. With eyes gray like flint and hard as steel,
he was unusual…beautiful…The intensity behind his gaze
made her feel like the only person in the world.
And then he whispers…

"I want your complete surrender."

Desert Me Now

DESIRE ME MORE

He was her lover…and her employer.

From the moment Amelia Grant accepted the position of secretary to Nicholas Riley, London's most notorious businessman, she knew her life would be changed forever. For Nick didn't just want her secretarial skills…he wanted her complete surrender.
And she was more than willing to give it to him, spending night after night in delicious sin. As the devastatingly insatiable Nick teaches her the ways of forbidden desire, Amelia begins to dream of a future together…

But in the light of day, sinister shadows lurk, determined to tear them apart.

ABOUT THE AUTHOR

Deciding that life had far more to offer than a nine-to-five job, bickering children, and housework of any kind (unless she's on a deadline when everything is magically spotless), **TIFFANY CLARE** opened up her laptop to write stories she could get lost in. Tiffany writes sexy historical romances set in the Victorian era. She lives in Toronto with her husband, two kids, and two dogs. You can find out more about her and her books at www.tiffanyclare.com.

Discover great authors, exclusive offers, and more at hc.com.